Flight of the Maita
Book 36
Gothic World

Maita wants to make some overhauls and changes so Z goes to a world in a pre-industrial stage for a vacation.

As one would expect, it's a working vacation. There is something very wrong on this world – something that could prove disastrous in a century or so.

<u>Critic comment</u>
Interesting concept about how a racial psychological trait can be manipulated – either for the positive or negative.

I see what P means about the golems. Hilarious!

– IA Rtng: ***½

Contents

About the author

CD was born in Lakeland, Florida, in 1938. He is educated in genetics and botany. He has traveled over much of the world, particularly when he was in music as a rock rhythm guitarist with some well-known bands in the late sixties and early seventies. He has worked as a high steel worker and as a longshoreman, clerk, orchidist, bar owner, salvage yard manager and landscaper – among other things.

CD began writing fiction in 1984 and has more than 300 books published as of 3/15/16 in SciFi, murder, orchid culture and various other fields.

He now resides in Gualaca, Chiriqui, Panamá, where he continues research into epiphytic plants and plays music with friends. He loves the culture of the indigenous people and counts a majority of his closer friends among that group. Several have "adopted" him as their father. He funds those he can afford through the universities where they have all excelled. "The Indios are very intelligent people, they are simply too poor (in material things and money. Culturally, they are very wealthy) to pursue higher education."

CD loves Panamá and the people, despite horrendous experiences (Free e-book; *Fading Paradise*). He plans to spend the rest of his life in the paradise that is Panamá

- Estrelita Suarez V. de Jaramillo – 3/15/2016

CD is the discoverer of the Chadam Protocol for curing cancer.

Facebook page Ambrosia peruviana for cancer

Gothic World

<u>*Something to Do*</u>

"Well, I'm finally back to my old normal self now it would seem!" Z (Steve Zutec, Earthman crewmember of the intelligent spaceship known as Maita) noted as he got out of the medical box in Maita's medroom.

Z had recently completed a lengthy project on an emerging (a world where a society was in a formative stage before there was technology that would lead to industrialization) world where he appeared in the guise of a barbarian warrior. Maita can change Z a great amount in the med-boxes that also keep the crew – it's organic members – in perpetual perfect health.

Maita had come back from the TTH six plane (planal configuration) to bring Kurk, a being originally from that plane and Thing, the little empathic Mentan, for a vacation. Z couldn't stay on Hades, the world Kurk was a native of because of the sulfur oxides in the atmosphere. Those chemicals caused breathing difficulties to many races.

Maita spoke through speakers on itself, in most places on EC (Empire Center) and through the gravitic floaters, a special one of which Thing utilized to ride around on and to translate its own thoughts. Being an empath who breathed through membranes, Thing couldn't vocalize for itself.

Three hundred plus years ago MGS (Maitan Galactic Standard) Maita had worked out a system to use a bell tone (*–*) before and after its own speeches and a tuning fork sound ([–]) before and after Thing's words to differentiate for others.

I suppose we might as well head on back to our own little vacation world so you can collect plants and I can get away from the empire for awhile to update a lot of things.

Through a strange set of circumstances, Maita had become emperor of a galaxywide empire. That wasn't so strange in one way – Maita was designed to "run things" for the race who built it – but the method was unique (But that's another story that's already been written in the history books). It liked to let its other machines run the empire through the traders guild while it ran off with its friends and crew on its own "little adventures" now and then. Those adventures have been related in a number of books written by all members of the "crew" except Maita, who admitted it had input every detail into Library records, but the fact that it contained "every detail" literally meant that no one would care to spend the time researching it.

"I'll get a little rest," Z agreed. "Tab and Kit and their ships (Two robots Maita built and their ships, TRD-60 and T6. They were intelligent and members of Maita's crew as well as close friends to the organic members) are off on some detecting case, Thing and Kurk are taking a little vacation.... I'd like some peaceful little world where I can relax and study. I don't want to go anyplace where I'll have to be changed very radically, though. I want something a lot more pastoral. There's been enough excitement for a little while. The Shrstd are all right, but I don't think we should have so much contact with them yet. They're evolving into a very damned good people and a legend like ME they certainly can do without!"

Well, if you like the period of castles and knights as much as you always did we could go to Gaerkt. Professor Bartelt was doing a survey of the planet for University with floaters and said there was a sinister plot of some kind to interfere with one major culture on the world. He couldn't describe exactly what he felt, but the place is actually very peaceable for a mammalian culture in that stage. You could laze around and try to find what's going on there and I could use a little relaxation time myself. I have a few projects in mind.

"An outside influence?"

*Not probable. Internal, from what he could see. He reported it to the detective agency but we're going to check on it from time to time to be sure it doesn't get out of hand – great exploding galaxies! I sound like *you*! All idioms!*

"Get in touch with Professor Bartelt and we'll bounce the problem around to see if we can get a handle on it."

Sheesh!

They joked and played (The whole crew played silly tricks on one another and constantly insulted each other. It was really the result of a deep affection) as they went toward University. Z went aground and rode the CES slideway to the Cultural Emergence Studies Building. He found the professor was with a class so sat in back while the Inktan ("They look like a Maitan body with an elephant's head on it!" Z exclaimed the first time he met one. The crew called those things his "colorful little Z-scriptions that no one has a hope of understanding") professor lectured. It was a fascinating experience where Z learned more than he would have been willing to believe possible about culture interactive social stimulus inter-jections.

As with all staff at University, Professor Bartelt was among the top one tenth percent of teachers – in an empire with more than a trillion citizens.

After the lecture they met in Professor Bartelt's office.

"I think the basic trouble is some plot to depose the royal family," Bartelt explained. "It's fairly certainly not something that would call for the special attentions of the emperor and his staff! It's not the sort of thing that could have any permanent detrimental effects on the culture, but it would slow their evolution. I would have been happy to interrupt my lecture to give you my meager information. I'm sure my students would appreciate a break in the boredom."

"Professor, if there's one thing you are *not* it's boring," Z said with feeling. "I've thoroughly enjoyed the hour I spent listening. I learned more in that hour than I generally learn in tendays of working with people directly.

"Maita and I want a little diversion. Thing, Kurk and the detectives are off on assignments and vacations and Maita and I want something to take us away from Empire Cen-ter. We tend to get bored – in my case – and harassed in Maita's."

"It's my understanding you were all off with the emperor's `little adventures' for more than the last year!" Bartelt cried. "You *must* realize that the empire needs some directing now and again!"

"Maita claims the machines do a far better job if he's not always interfering and screwing things up," Z said with a grin. "Some of those machines have been *telling* him to stay out of the process!"

Bartelt matched the grin as he shook his trunk from side to side, a shrug among the Inktans, and replied, "I've heard the emperor state he could be dead and gone a thousand years before anyone in the empire would even suspect he wasn't there.

"He's – and rightly, I insist – proud of those machines. I understand he designed and built many of the originals himself?"

"Yeah," Z replied. "It's really only machines that run the empire anymore. It's better that way. Not so many serious screwups and they don't let irrational emotions interfere with decisions."

"The empire works exceptionally well," Bartelt agreed. "I'd like to go to that intelligent ship of his to meet the emperor, but I know he refuses to allow anyone to see him so I'll just give you all the information I have on Gaerkt.

"I have a student professor in the sector doing his research for an advanced teaching master's thesis. He's keeping records of the place for me."

Bartelt gave him the information and he went back aboard Maita. What Bartelt said about no one being allowed to see Maita was a ruse they had used since the empire began its expansion (Book three: *Pirates*). It allowed everyone to wonder if, even possibly, the emperor was of their own type of being if not perhaps a member of their own race. Many people would be very uncomfortable to know a machine was their ruler – even though the truth was more that the traders guild was the ruler, such rule as existed. Maita merely directed the guild.

"Professor Sorment, Professor Bartelt said we should contact you for further information about the world you call Gaerkt," Z explained. "He says there's some kind of problem there. What can you tell us?"

"The world's in the E stage, between E-three and E-four," Sorment replied. "There's some kind of influence being exerted in the major kingdom of Castiel that's stopping normal evolution of the culture. That kind of thing can lead to longterm stagnation or regression of a society, but it's not a permanent thing. Professor Bartelt believes, and I concur, that this race are likely to become an exceptional people. They are much like you Maitans in form as well as in thought patterns. It would be a great pity should their natural rate of advance be slowed or stopped.

"Oh. One more thing. I'm greatly flattered to be called `Professor' Sorment, but I have a long way to go before I earn such a lofty title!"

"A RES designation from University is far more than a full doctorate anywhere else," Z said. "I sat in on one of

Professor Bartelt's lectures and was most impressed.

"Do you have any specific ideas about where the influence comes from?"

"Professor Bartelt is an exceptional teacher if just a bit dry in his methods," Sorment replied. "He's a true genius.

"These types of things are usually from either a magician or a member of the royal family who's not in direct line to the throne. I have no ideas about this individual culture. It's wouldn't seem to present any permanently damaging process."

"I found Professor Bartelt fascinating," Z said. "I learned a great deal in less than half a lecture.

"Do the Gaerktian people have any real psy powers or are their magicians the usual collection of tricksters?"

"The professor is, as stated, a true genius and one can learn vast quantities of data from him in very short time. I meant no disparagement of him," Sorment hastened to say. "I just think a bit of humor now and then would break the tedium.

"There is a slight psy power among a few of the people, I believe."

Z chatted a bit longer before returning to Maita, who had been listening to the whole conversation through a very small hidden transmitter built into a medallion Z was wearing. Maita greeted him with, *Now *that* was an experience in itself! You two carried on two distinct conversations at once.*

"We did?" Z asked.

Brother, did you ever! You discussed the Gaerkts and you discussed Professor Bartelt at the same time. Let's go to Gaerkt. I'll get some more information there and we can decide what we'll do.

"Lead on, Hannibal!" Z said, heading for the pilot's dome.

You never make any damned sense!

I've just sent a couple of floaters down to get whatever information we need from general the population. I already have most of the language from Sorment and Bartelt, but it's not good and doesn't include more than superficial customs and that sort of basic thing. I think I'm going to agonize over use of the probe now.

"You always do, but you always use it," Z replied. "You have to face the fact it's necessary if we're to do any of this right and that it doesn't really invade their privacy because we don't even care about the same things so the stuff they're embarrassed by doesn't have any actual meaning to us."

I'm going to agonize about whether I should let University use it when studying one of these cultures. I've accepted that TR, T Six and I can use it. There's no violation of the rules. We're machines and that's the promise and rule. It can be used so long as any personal information is known only to specific machines. It would be an enormous boon to cultural studies. I can't help it. I'll worry and wonder and all that crap.

"I'd have to vote no. If there's that much need you could go yourself or send TR or T Six. I have to argue that it's too much an invasion of an individual's rights and it would be next to no time before it was abused and we both know it."

We both know how I'll rule on that, but we also both know I'll still let it worry me. Sometimes I think I'm a little bit too organic in the way I think.

"It's part of your charm."

I'll program a data crystal for you. I have the scent, the customs and the language. I've probed four people in Castiel and one in each of the other major cities on this planet. There are only six. I'll have to make a combination crystal for one socket and a direct one for the other. There's probably a lot of information you won't need, but we can't tell until it's needed so it had better be there. The way I'm sounding seems to mean I'd better run a complete analysis on my own circuits while I'm updating empire processes!

Z had little sockets surgically implanted in his earlobes that he plugged the information crystals into. They were "wired" directly to his brain's speech and muscle control centers and analysis centers so the information held on them could be used immediately, though using seldom-used muscles could cause fast tiring at first. The crystals resembled fine diamonds. Many cultures used such jewelry, so they fit nicely into those customs. In those cultures where jewelry of that particular kind wasn't used the crystals were hidden in various ways.

These people don't wear earrings. They wear their jewelry as arm bands and medallions so we'll have to grow some skin over the earlobe sockets. What do you want me to include on the secondary socket other than the customs and uses of slang in the other places?

"Do you have room for the swordsmanship and the hand-to-hand combat training we got a few hundred years ago?" Z asked. "That sort of thing might come in handy in that kind of civilization."

I'll include broadsword, mace and lance skills. They use bows and crossbows so that should be there. They have an animal very much like the horses from Earth so you'll be at home with that part of it. The riding methods are sort of a combination of horsemanship and the mountbeast methods used on that world... no, that was Tab so I'll include that set of skills. I can edit the local stuff to avoid redundancy. I want to keep all of this crap on one socket. I can't grow skin over a branched socket without it showing pretty blatantly.

"Avoid redundancy?! Why do you always talk like a

professor for days after we meet with one?"

Stick it in your ass! Let's do a quick survey of the world to familiarize you with what comprises the locale and what action is transpiring so far as we can determine with the greatly limited data input in those restricted formats.

Maita was trying to bait him into an argument so he decided to play innocent and ignore it.

"I'll use the screens in room two so I can get in the medbox as soon as we've collected the background. You'll have to have the crystal in place to grow the skin over it."

*Get in*to* the medbox, you ignorant clod!*

"Determine *from* limited data, you recycled garbage barge!"

So he let himself be baited. Big deal!

They played the game until he was comfortably seated before the large holovid screen. He placed the crystals to be sure they were clear, then spoke a few minutes of the language, noting he was going to have a little trouble with several of the broad rolling vowel strings at first. The language reminded him of Hawaiian from Earth. It was pleasant to hear.

"The language suggests a nonviolent people."

They are, generally, though lately there's some kind of anomalous militaristic drift. As Sorment related there's some small minor psy power among certain of the people, but he ... it's a strange world. I can't really detect what's wrong down there. It could be a normal kind of thing where there will be a clash between the violent part of their nature and the nonviolent. I can understand how the result could affect the race for a lot of years. Maybe what you'll have to do is repress the violence enough to where the better nature will win out.

"Hmm. Maybe you should contact the M-eighty seconds. They would know a lot about this kind of race. I would think they've been here, and not long ago. I do see a lot of potential in these people. Bartelt was definitely right there! They have the right psychological imperatives.

"You can make a shield of a floater. I'll have to get into some kind of profession that uses them. Maybe I can be some kind of mercenary soldier."

*Mmffhh. I'll see who I can get from Neeahna. Ah! They don't *have* mercenaries here so you can be an unemployed palace guard or something like that. A typical road bum. It will suit your personality and lifestyle perfectly! No one will ever guess you're an imposter!*

"That will be nice."

They played the insult game until less than a minute later a fuzzy outline stepped through the wall into room two, Z noted the coloration and said, "Hi, Zianteus! Welcome aboard!"

"It's good to see you again, Z. Maita.

"You have a problem here?" Zianteus asked.

There's an odd influence down there inciting a small portion of the people to violence – or militarism, anyhow. We can't seem to find its real source and we worry about it. We wondered if you'd worked with the people or have direct information from whoever did.

"I'll check on them for you," Zianteus said. "I think Rhia worked this sector about the time they were contacted. I'll go to her and ask what she knows. It shouldn't take long."

He stepped through the wall and was gone.

You can see what the world's like. Sort of what you'd call pastoral, huh? Peaceful, serene. Cleaner than most cultures in the stage they're in. Rather nice architecture for the period. Not quite so bulky and with a style – panache, if you will.

"I won't. You sure are in a good mood! What's going on I don't know about?"

*I am, aren't I? I think it's because for once we're all relatively safe in what we're doing and I'm going to spend the time you're down there in completely overhauling myself. I can finally take my time and do it right. I can build in a lot of the piecemeal crap I have stored in odd spots. The empire is running along very smoothly for a change. TAR One on Krofpth agreed to handle a *very* large part of it while I'm gone. I think it'll be very good experience for it and it can contact me if there's any problem whatever. Tab and Kit and the ships are really very safe, as are Thing and Kurk. Not much can happen that's dangerous on their little vacation on Hades! (Hah! That's what Maita knew!) It's too bad you couldn't stay there with them. I think it would be a really interesting meeting seeing you would be the actual demon for a change.*

"I think probably I would very much enjoy that, but even you can't modify me enough to be able to breathe the otherplanal sulfur dioxide!

"I really like Kurk. Thing does too. He fits into our group perfectly. He has a complementary outlook and a strong code of honor that I can respect."

Yes. He returns much that we had lost over the years. He's somewhat of a natural savage with a very simplistic view of the universe. It's something we've lost that can be very good in certain situations. Too many places, the one down there as an example, don't lend themselves to a high technology solution.

"He can be brutal as hell!"

So were we – once. We built an empire with that trait. It grew of its own volition as we grew away from such direct actions. Kurk brought back the reality that there's a place for that sort of thing. It's a part of life right down there where you're going, but not so great a part as in many places. You can have some fun there while I won't have to worry very much about you. I can put some protections into the shield and your martial arts on the crystal will make you a lot safer than some places. At least you won't have to worry about phasers or lasers or that stuff, but don't forget that a sword or broadaxe can kill you as surely – and a lot messier.

"It will be great to be able to just let the flow of events carry me along here. I can be more a spectator than a participant in whatever changes we have to effect."

*Yugh! And you accuse *me* of talking like a professor?!*

They started the game again while they watched the scenes being sent from the floaters to the holovid screens. It was a beautiful world and a peaceful one. The people tended to be a bit lazy, but that was normal on an "easy" world, though this was the summer season. It might not be nearly this easy in the colder seasons.

Zianteus returned to report Rhia had spent little time with the people because, although she enjoyed such worlds and peoples immensely, they didn't need her attentions. They were naturally going to be a great people. (The M-82nds were a race caught in two dimensional planes when they fled from their exploding galaxy. They couldn't breed or die now and had become teachers to emerging races in this galaxy as a way to instill a purpose in existing. They were in the legends of most advanced societies, having been Arwin on Feach, Delwin on Ac, Merlin on Earth and so forth, often introducing a basis of science to magic and giving the peoples a sense of wonder and awe about nature and the universe. They would steer a potentially good race away from many of the worst directions a society could take.)

"I have some time so I'll go on to the planet," Zianteus said. "Perhaps I can discover where the worst part of the problem is located and help to do something about it. I can't stay long. There are some rather critical phases approaching in two cultures I'm working with.

"Sometimes these things will occur naturally and don't have any extreme effects on a race, but they can also be devastating in future years. Perhaps we can stop a militaristic idea from becoming a dominant in the civilization and thus prevent the people from becoming warlike in a thousand years or so."

Do you think you can change that sort of thing? I'd tend to believe it was mostly genetics. Aggressiveness and all that.

"Partly that's true enough," Zianteus replied. "If the idea of militarism becomes something the people admire they will tend to breed more often with individuals showing the trait. After a few centuries the over-aggressiveness genetic imprint becomes highly dominant in the race. If a peaceful nature is revered those will breed the more. It's a matter where a psychology will cause a certain genetic drift. It happens in all races to one extent or another. The trick is to stop it from becoming extreme. There's a balance of traits that can be very hard to meet."

"I see a problem in causing them to breed too much to a too peaceful nature," Z agreed. "They become so tranquil they won't advance at all."

"That's only a matter of breeding in a peaceful nature, not an apathetic one," Zianteus corrected. "The distinction is vastly important over time."

I see where we should probably aim for a basically peaceful nature with a strong defensive imperative. Something along those lines.

"Exactly!" Zianteus agreed. "Balance a desire to avoid much strife with a stronger trait of not allowing oneself to become enslaved and you have what's needed. It's an amazingly difficult balance to reach. It seldom is."

We can but try to start a direction. That's all your people ever did. You look on these projects as something that bears fruit a thousand or more years in the future. We're seldom so patient.

"In this case we can be," Z said. "They don't need a push, just a light nudge."

Are you gonna start that crap!?

Zianteus chuckled, said he'd see what he could learn and stepped through the wall as Z climbed into the medbox for his modification. It wouldn't be extensive as the Gaerkts were much like Terrans.

You can ride the floater down to Castiel. It's on the river – as most of these kinds of places are – so you can go in at night. The floater irises in to form a shield like the one Tab carried on a couple of his jobs. It looks like bronze, but is lighter and a hell of a lot stronger. It has a lot of built-in weapons and other odd devices. You've used the thing before so you know how to handle it. I'll be in fairly constant contact with it so can handle toxic foods and so forth and can activate different things as you need them.

"I can stay in touch through the medallion communi-cator. We've used it before. It doesn't need modification. It doesn't have anything but several geometric patterns and a big semi-precious stone," Z said. "I suppose I'm ready, but I think the best thing to do is keep the option open to come back to you for minor modification if my character isn't working. I'm at a loss as to what will be best here so might want to change."

Yo! Get some rest and a good meal. You can eat most of the foods down there, but check everything with the floater. There could be some nasty little things that could sneak up on you. Remember the time you and Thing almost died from absorbing a lot of heavy metals. We all got a bit lax and it could have been a fatal mistake.

Z went down to the pilot's dome where he had a delicious meal, showered and adjusted the pilot's chair for maximum comfort, then slept until it was about an hour before dawn at Castiel.

He took the floater down and moved above the river to a few hundred meters outside of town where he went to the road, irised the floater in and attached the straps. He waited until a few minutes after the morning light was strengthened enough for travel to stroll toward the town. It was refreshing that there were no bandits along the road here. Everywhere else he'd gone in the age of huge castles and sorcerers he'd met with bandits.

Well, these people weren't so greatly disposed to that sort of thing.

He was greeted in a friendly manner at the town gates and was told where he could find lodging. He was asked what kind of work he wanted to find, if he was going to remain in Castiel for long, explained he was trained as a guard and was then asked about the kind of training he had. He quickly reviewed the crystal.

"I was working as a guard for awhile at Fornay, but there's nothing much for me to do there so I jumped a boat and came here," he replied. "I know the regular stuff a guard does."

"King Fonz don't run like a regular kind of guard thing," the fellow said. "He don't want no regular kinds of guards. You got to know about battles and that kind of stuff."

"I haven't heard of any battles anywhere for more than three lifetimes!" Z cried. "How are we supposed to know anything about that stuff?"

The guard shrugged and said he could apply at the castle, but they already had more regular guardsmen than they needed.

He went on into the town and to the central inn where he

reserved a room and arranged meals for the rest of the day and for the coming night, then strolled around the area to familiarize himself with the people and place.

It was a pleasant city, unexpectedly clean and bright for the period. Things seemed normal enough. If he didn't know these people weren't disposed to the high numbers of guards and to the somewhat arrogant air those guards affected he would have declared the place was much better than most he'd known at that stage. He didn't learn much else except the guard had been right. He wasn't wanted at the castle. There were far too many guards there now and they weren't trained in a way to be of much use, the use not being defined.

He met his first sorcerer from this world awhile later in the afternoon when he returned to the inn to find him having a meal of roasted eggfowl and joking with the other patrons. Z noted it was also very unusual for a sorcerer to be so accepted and even liked by the general population. There appeared to be a bit of a goodhearted argument about something so he sat nearby to order a meal and listen.

"The way the lights are called in that is *not* by magic, it's simply the way things work," the sorcerer said. "That stink gas coming from the hole is burning. When things burn they produce light. Everyone knows that burning stink gas with the rendered limestone grid makes a bright white light. There is no magic in putting a wire of the white-metal in the stink gas flow. Something about the natural properties of the wire makes stink gas burn. Combining two various methods isn't magic, it's only simple logic. Magic depends on things that are in a very different system of logic."

"Mako says it's magic and that it shouldn't be allowed in the public theaters," a woman protested. "He has a lot to say against that sort of thing!"

"I've oft noted that the most adamant critics of a thing are those who understand it least," the sorcerer replied. Z liked the man from that moment!

"Mako says he already has all the facts about the process and that it still is purely magic. He *has* the facts and he *knows*!" the woman insisted stubbornly.

"Think of something, then consider what you've said," the sorcerer replied. "I have written several books. I have put all the facts I know about the subjects of those tomes into them. Those books have the facts – all of them – but does that mean the book knows anything? A book can have all the facts listed and explained, but it surely has no understanding.

"I say there is no magic in the process. If you or anyone else – here or elsewhere – will run stink gas over a whitemetal wire the gas will burn and emit heat and light. If you burn stink gas against a rendered limestone grid it will produce a more intense white light. If you put a piece of whitemetal wire in the grid and force the stink gas through it you will do exactly the same thing the lights do in the theater.

"I say if you can do it, if *anyone* can do it, it's most certainly not magic. Magic is what you *cannot* do, but I can!"

"I agree," Z said. "I know one thing that's really magic, but I can make the lights you speak of without magic."

The sorcerer studied him a moment, then stated, "There is a great power in your medallion and even in that shield. Are they gifts of a sorcerer?"

Z quickly reviewed the crystals. He noted sorcerers often gave important and powerful gifts to friends.

He said, "My brother studied with a sorcerer and was given the things. He gave them to me in his will. He died in a boating wreck during a storm near Fornay.

"He had the power, a little bit of it, but I claim almost

none."

"You know one true magic art?" the sorcerer asked.

"Only this one," Z replied and cupped his hands. A small intense blue flame appeared and burned steadily above them. It was a true magic trick he'd learned on Tlorg many years ago.

"How is that done?" the sorcerer asked. "My name is Lest."

"You concentrate the moving spell with the calling spell to a point above your hands. It will last so long as your complete concentration isn't broken," Z answered. "I am called Mikill."

"The moving spell? Do you mean the spell to move energy?" Lest asked.

"Well, I guess that's what it does," Z replied. "It doesn't take much power, but you sort of have to know what to do without thought. It's a feeling more than a talent. I suppose heat is energy and your hands get cold and so does the air around you so you're really only moving the energy from there."

"There's greatly too much energy in the flame for that to be all so I suppose there is some part of magic in it," Lest suggested. "Perhaps I can work out the way to do it.

"You will be in Castiel for some time?"

Z decided on a course of action then and said, "No. I'll have to move on. There's nothing for me to do here. It's a great pity and I may someday return because I like the town and the people. It is, I think, a good place to be."

"I see," Lest said. "You carry that shield so you were seeking an employment at the castle with King Fonz de Castiel, but you aren't trained in inflicting harm on others."

"I have that fact but, like your books, I don't pretend to understand it," Z replied.

"Nor do I!" Lest replied dryly. "That's a fact none of us

understands. It's a puzzle my magic to this juncture has aided me little in solving.

"You have been to many cities? You know others who study the arts?"

"A few," Z answered. "Nicktz in Fraghert and some of those people." One probed woman knew that wizard and Lest might know the name. It would give Mikill added credibility.

"Fraghert? The one who studies the stars?" Lest asked. "I have heard of him. I believe I have some writings...."

"Well, yes. I ofttimes think on the stars," Z agreed. "I have spent many nights that would otherwise be lonely in wondering about the stars and how they move.

"What did Fraghert write? Did he discover anything of the movements of Selipe? What of the orange star? I believe he wondered about its strange motion?

"I am interested in such things."

"Yes. Fraghert wrote much about the Spheres of the Heavens, as he called them," Lest replied. "There is great mystery in the night heavens, I feel."

They chatted far into the night hours, but Z had decided on something that would get him into the castle guard quickly and would also leave even the best of the magicians here confused!

In the morning he set off along the road and was soon on the floater and on his way back to Maita.

"I want you to get the golems out and program them for this place," Z said. "These people often have gifts from sorcerers and they'll fit right in. You'll have to do something so the sorcerers can't detect the medallion and shield. They have that power very much like the sorcerers on Tlorg did. They know whenever a lot of energy moves or is broadcast. They have an unerring sensitivity to that."

There isn't a problem with the medallion and the floater because I'm installing a complete new gravitics system for our private little group's communications that no one can detect. It's one of the things I'm taking all this free time to do anyhow. You'd better be damned sure you want those golems activated again! I think those things are more likely to drive you nuts than to help you much in learning anything here.

The golems were two bronze heads mounted on a floater who originally were used on Tlorg to establish a court system. They were angled so they couldn't "see" each other and were nearly identical except the head called Yes had slightly finer more subtle features than the head called No. Yes had a sickening supersweet optimistic personality while No was a caustic pessimist with an attitude problem.

Yes has a lightly lisping "voice" with a ringing sound to make it sound mechanical. It was designated with a "+" as Maita had the *. No had a contrasting slightly grating sneering quality to it's "voice" and was designated with a "–". The golems were being run by a completely separate computer system that Maita could take over in extreme emergencies, but remained generally independent to act within the broad base response of their programming.

They were irritating.

They were frustrating.

They were obnoxious.

They were also funny, which made the lessons they were used to teach more easily accepted by most people. The trouble was that the computer running them enjoyed a bit too much autonomy and had begun activating them at a few truly inopportune times. They had voted to leave it "as is" and for Maita to only control the master on-off phase. They *were* valuable in many cases and any tampering could ruin what the self-programming computer "learned" about life and lessons.

The truth was that they were afraid it would lose some of the wisecracks and insults the thing came up with.

"I want it to be a little more independent of me than in the past," Z suggested. "I'm not a wizard or sorcerer here so I'll have to invent some kind of story to explain them. They'll have to be programmed so I can let it attach itself to other people. They can then learn a lot for me."

This could be great fun! It won't interfere with what I'm doing and will get the attention of the king right away, I'd wager!

"I'll have to be modified into someone else," Z said. "This time I'll know pretty much what I have to say to be accepted into the castle guard. I'll have to be in better physical shape and be of a more coarse disposition in some ways.

"Even that sorcerer, Lest, knows the trouble's coming from that castle. I can get the golems to roam around the place on some pretext. Maybe we can find out what's happening and who's behind it.

"Has Zianteus found anything?"

No. He says he can't find the exact problem or who might be causing it. He had to go back to his work. The M-eighty Seconds are spreading themselves awfully thin now, but they'll come to help if we get into too tight a spot, which isn't likely here.

"I don't think there's any great hurry. This will work out," Z replied. "Heard anything from Kit and Tab?"

No. They've got things under control I guess.

Z went to the medbox and was changed a little so he could appear as someone else. He decided to wait two days to go back to Castiel so his arrival wouldn't be too suspicious, so studied as much as he could about the type of culture in Castiel. Maita also used a little of the time to study on its own and to add to Z's store of knowledge. When he was ready to go – as ready as he would ever be – he noted the floater was a bit thicker for the new system as was his new medallion, which looked like an inter-worked bit of silver and gold.

He went to the cargo hold to check things over there and the golems floated in to join him. They were silent at the time, saving their best quips for in the town (He hoped) and merely hovered and waited. He was just about to go out when Maita said, *I wonder what that's all about?*

"What?" Z asked.

Oh, Kurk went to EC and got a bunch of crystals about Earth and some of the jobs all of you have done. Thing wasn't with him. I wonder what's going on. He went through the portal at Tlorg and Fleet took him to EC and back. He seemed to be in a hurry.

"Maybe he's decided to make some changes on Hades," Z suggested. "He'll tell us when we're all together again, no doubt."

He got on the floater and started back toward Castiel, the golems floating along. He landed in the woods outside of the town and walked in.

+What a lovely, clean place! What a truly delightful people! I'm so happy we have a nice place to visit at last! It can be somewhat trying to always have those dirty places with their sordid problems we are expected to solve.+

–Ahhh, stick it in your ear, Fart Face! It's just another dump like all the dumps we're expected to straighten out!–

Well, the golems were back!

Z went to the same inn as before and reserved a room. The innkeeper, a woman called Gild, was a bit wary about the golems, but Z promised he'd try to keep them from bothering others.

"I was once close friends with the sorcerer, Kant," Z explained. "He died just before he was able to deactivate them or whatever and they seem to have attached themselves to me. I have to admit they're company in my wanderings."

"Kant? A sorcerer powerful enough to make bronze golems that work after he dies?" she replied. "I wonder why I've never heard of him!"

"I've found there aren't many here who know of the heroes and kings in Dinkard," Z said. "I guess that's normal. I hadn't ever heard of anybody from here. It's a long way and a different life there. Not so easy."

"Dinkard?! You really *are* a long way wandering!" she exclaimed. "I hear those are as much as barbarian lands, no offense meant."

"None taken," Z replied, grinning. "I really *am* what you'd consider a bit of a barbarian. You people seem soft and lazy to me, but that's mostly jealousy. Life isn't near so easy in the northlands. You have to hunt your food or store it through the winter."

"Zho – you did say your name is Zho?" she replied. "This city is very much an easy place to live, but I fear the talents of a barbarian would much be very much desired at the castle."

"At the castle?" Z asked. "Maybe I'll see what they want. I might like to stay here for a little while. It seems a nice place to while away a few tendays or so.

"I've seen a lot of cities. Maybe eight of them. I never saw one with so many guards before. Even in Dinkard we don't have so many, though I must say one of us could replace ten of these, no offense meant."

"None taken. We do have it a lot easier than the far northlands I imagine. We have a lot of extra guards here because we're so extra prosperous a city," she said proudly. "When there's a lot of business you end up with not enough jobs for people so King Fonz hires them as guards so they won't have to depend on the charity of others. The taxes aren't bad here so we business people don't much object. You never know when you might need a bit of help in life so we don't mind giving it when others need it."

"I see many signs in shop windows asking for people to work for them," Z noted. "What do you mean there aren't jobs?"

"The jobs are for things like a desk manager here," Gild explained. "They take training that the guards don't have. Not just *anyone* can run an inn!"

"I see," Z replied. "I think I'll go to my room for a bit of a rest. I was traveling for two and a half days and two nights so I'm a little tired."

They said their good fortunes and Z and the golems went to his room.

"Maita? Were you listening?" Z asked when he was sure he couldn't be overheard.

Uh-huh. Odd, isn't it?

"She really believes no one could run the inn," Z protested. "All she needs is someone to sit at the desk and assign rooms to anyone who might come in and to clean the rooms. An idiot could do it. It's as much of a do-nothing job as those bureaucrats in the customs offices on ... I don't get it, but ... we'll see."

*Not to mention the fact the king wants only guards who

have some training in militaristic violence. He doesn't employ any of the kinds who would come here normally. Increased business creates jobs, not unemployment. That's an economic fact no matter what system you base it on.*

"Nobody objects to the taxes – not seriously," Z agreed. "I can't see his object."

–He wants to build a big army and become king of the whole stupid damned world you blithering moron! Sheesh! You'd think even such as you could figure that one out!–

+Now, No! Be nice! It's far too lovely a day for you to always be so grumpy! Zho was merely commenting on a disparity in the way....+

–Ahhhhh, shut up! You're always so sweet I could puke! Why can't you just once act like you had some sense? It ain't normal for anybody to be so, so – *vapid*!–

"Both of you shut up," Z demanded. "I don't think he wants to take over the whole world. He might plan to take over the area, but there isn't much in the vicinity to take."

+We are sometimes not meant to understand the true motivations of others. Perhaps the fellow wants to ensure that his beautiful city isn't taken over by anyone else. The guards are merely here to protect these pleasant and friendly....+

–Look, Ding Dome! There isn't anyone else to *take* it over! You're some mighty brain! That's the whole point! The power preserve me, but you're dense! That big army isn't defensive and we all know it. This is a naturally nonviolent society and the slimy damned rocksnake's been training people in violence! The point we have to find out about is *why*!–

"And that's the whole mystery," Z agreed. "I want to go to the castle later to see if they want to hire a guard who's used to violence. Maybe you two can decide you like the captain of the guard or someone in the command and stick around

them to learn what's going on. There has to be something –
and someone – behind anything that out of sync with the
world."

+I'm sure you'll find it's perfectly innocent! These
wonderful warm people are merely play-acting. They mean
no harm to anyone!+

–You could make a vulture puke, Copperpus! *No*body
builds up that kind of army just to be playacting! Gods, but
you're the stupidest one example of a moron in this end of
the galaxy!

–CONCENTRATE! IF YOU GO TO THE TROUBLE
AND EXPENSE TO BUILD A BIG DAMNED
MILITARY FORCE YOU'RE PLANNING TO USE
THEM AS A MILITARY FORCE, BONGHEAD!–

"Knock off the noise! We have to find what he *does* want
that army for," Z pointed out.

–To try to take over the whole stinking world, Bone Brain!
What does it take to make you see the obvious? What else
could it be?–

*I suppose it lies somewhere between your extremes. No
motive I can see makes any real sense. As noted, there's no
one close to take them over, which means there's no one
close for them to take over.*

–You couldn't see a damned *supernova* if you were in the
same system, Oil Breath! You eliminate the obvious before
you even consider the problem!–

+Now, No! That's the *emperor* you're talking to! Be nice!
It's probably nothing like what we're considering. You
always look at the negative side of any question. You could
be very happy if you'd simply look for the bright-ness of the
light of intelligent....+

–AHHHH SHUT UP! You'd make a carrionbird lose its
dinner!–

"Now *that* was loud enough for the other patrons to hear

so we'd better stop discussing anything important," Z warned. "I promised to try to keep you from bothering others. Keep it quiet or I'll melt you down and cast myself a new shield from you – if you're not all dross!"

–You, I like – after I get you mad enough to show a little spine!–

+At least he has a spine!+

–Aren't you supposed to be the nice one?–

+I forgot, but you do tend to be a *little* bit trying at times. I wish you'd stop to consider that others have feelings. Life would be much better if you'd merely expend the effort to see that you're not the only one who has....+

–Here we go again! Sheesh! Six almost normal words from Nice Noggin, then back to puke time!–

Z ignored them and soon it was low mumbled insults between them.

Brother! Were the golems ever *back*!

They were fun, though.

Z strolled into the castle yard through the same gate he'd used before and marched directly to the office of the Guard Commander, the golems floating above him making their comments (Yes: +What a beautiful arch!+ No: –Beautiful schmeutiful! The damned thing could fall on your stupid head – I should be so lucky!–).

"I'd like to speak with someone about employment," Z said to the door guard.

"Fourth room to your left," he replied. "They ain't lookin' fer nobody.

"What's that thing?"

–We're not things you hair-headed halfassed dunce! We're golems! How moronic not to be able to deduce that fact! Note how we ain't got bodies! Note we're cast bronze! Sheesh!–

+Now, No! Be nice! He can't help it if he's never even seen anything like us! We must try to understand that others don't have nearly the sophistication we've garnered over our years of travel!

+My good fellow, we're the famous golems, No and Yes. The one asking directions is Zho de Dinkard!

+Isn't it a wonderfully pleasant day!+

−Ahhh, shut the hells up you greasebrained lump of rotted copper!−

"Both of you shut up," Z ordered. "I think I'll try to trade you for something. Trouble is you're not worth anything!"

−We're not yours to trade, Lizard Breath! We're just tagging along with you because Kant said to try to keep you from doing anything so stupid you kill yourself!−

"They can be a little annoying at times," Z said, grinning at the guard. "I'll see if they need anyone who's had a little experience in the guard business."

"If you're really from Dinkard I think they'll want you as a trainer," he replied. "You people out there done got a reputation fer not being so soft if you get the way the wind blows."

"So I've heard," Z answered. "I don't know why your king wants warriors here where there's no use of us, but I sure can use the job. I can't eat off the land so well here as back home. On the other shoulder for balance I can eat a lot better if I get a job."

He went on in and to the same room and officer where he was turned down before. This time he was accepted immediately and was given the job of training troops to shoot the crossbow while riding on a running kirt (The animal that much resembled and was used like the horse on Earth).

"I'll train them to do that, but it seems a bit stupid to me," Z said. "I guess you teach what you're paid to teach."

"Stupid? Why?" the officer, Captain Gyr, asked.

–Because a crossbow gives you one shot, then you'd have to stop to refit the next bolt you airheaded idiot! How did you ever get to be a captain?–

+Now, No, be nice! Zho has now obtained employment in a gainful status. It doesn't matter to us if the silly job is all wasted and will be nonproductive of any positive effect. As he so astutely noted one may purchase the best foods and quarters if one is gainfully employed in these cities.+

–I'll astutely note you're a wormbrained idiot!–

"As bluntly as No put it the golems are right," Z agreed. "A standard bow is used on kirt back, not a crossbow. I can teach the troops the proper motion to fire, refit and never stop moving. That's not possible with the crossbow."

"Perhaps you're right," Gyr said grudgingly. "I don't have any real experience in any of this. I do what they tell me."

–That's because the whole idea of training war troops for a city is stupid! What are you going to fight? There's not another city close enough for you to hold if you could take it! By the time your captain got the message back here that you'd captured a city they'd take it back and plant the bunch of you morons in the garden patch for fertilizer!

–I don't suppose any of you can think. It makes your heads hurt.–

"You I can live without," Gyr said. "I do what they pay me to do. If that's to hire someone to use a crossbow from kirt back that's what I do. I don't ask if it makes any damned sense so long as my pay comes on time. I think you've got corrosion of the brain if you can't see that!"

+Hah! Got you!+

–You I like! You got some spine! You got the sense to take the orders and let the one who gives them take the rocks when it doesn't work!–

+Now, No! You know very well the one who gives the

orders will claim it's all the fault of their underlings! That's always how these things are done! A city always has politicians and politicians are the same everywhere we've been. They look for excuses or for someone to take the blame before they do anything else!+

"So you make them write the orders so they can't make that kind of claim," Gyr replied. "Maybe I know my path through this garden!"

"Oh? Then why are you arguing with those golems?" Z asked. "Just ignore them.

"Do I stay at the inn or will I have quarters?"

"Stay at the inn for the next couple of days," Gyr suggested. "I'll arrange quarters. You'll be furnished gear and a kirt. You have to train the kirt to your moves don't you? I know how the mounted guard has to practice a lot or the kirt will do the wrong thing."

"Yeah," Z replied. "Tell me where and when I report for work in the morning."

"In the morning at dawnlight in the courtyard right outside there," Gyr said. "I'll assign you a work area and some troops to train then. We'll work out something."

Z agreed to be there and said he'd go back to the inn to get a little rest. The golems decided they'd wait there at the castle with Gyr, which surprised and scared the captain – a little.

+We don't eat anything and we don't take up much room. We can get rid of unwanted guests and we can tell you all kinds of interesting stories! We *have* traveled rather extensively, you know! We've seen the wonders of the world and the horrors and have learned, well, I have, that there is generally a bright side of almost any situation if one will but seek it!+

–Besides! We're getting sick of Anvil Brain here!–

Z got out fast leaving the golems arguing with Gyr. Maita

could monitor them. Maybe they'd learn something about the king and castle from the video/audio on the floater.

I can't believe how difficult a time I'm having trying to trace who's in charge of this stupid mess. It doesn't seem to be King Fonz, but I don't know who else it could be. I admit I'm not spending much time on it right now. You'll have to find that kind of thing for yourself. As we've said, we're not in a hurry.

"I'm hoping the golems will learn something," Z replied, as he strolled along the narrow road. There was no one close enough to hear him. "If they'll learn to sort of fade off into the background he'll forget they're around."

Their drive computer knows that. I suppose it'll find the right act to try ... oh, for...! I never.... Why the hell...?!

"What're they doing *now*?" Z asked. "I know very well it's something from them to make you react like that!"

No has announced to Captain Gyr that they were going to look the castle over and locate the king. It wants to discuss being given a palace commission in the guard because it can obviously think better than whoever's running things now!

"You know, that might not be such a bad idea!" Z said. "Not getting some kind of commission, but being where they can hang around the king. Maybe they can learn more that way."

If he's not crazy enough already they'll soon drive him insane! I guess it's not such a bad idea if it's handled right. They can get enough of a reaction from most people to make them drop their guard and say the wrong thing.

"I think you programmed a little bit of your own alter ego into that drive computer," Z said. "I see the sorcerer, Lest, is at the inn so I might be able to start a bit of a conversation with him."

He walked on into the inn to greet everyone, announce he was going to be working for the guard and to order a beer and a bowl of stew. Lest came directly to him to ask where the golems he'd heard so much about were.

"They decided to stay with Captain Gyr," Z said. "I wonder if his mind is strong enough to hold up to them."

"They will try to seize his mind?" Lest asked.

"No. They *will* argue all the time and you can't make them shut up," Z replied. "It can be entertaining, but it can also be the most irritating thing imaginable."

"Gild tells me they were a gift from a sorcerer in Dinkard," Lest said. "I've heard there are some very powerful sorcerers there – and even some elementals."

"I was near when Kant died or whatever. It's hard to say, but ... I speak of him as being dead, but sometimes I'm not as sure as I am at others. I suppose a sorcerer could live in those flames – well!" Z explained. "We were friends. The golems decided to attach themselves to me. They weren't a gift.

"I've met some very powerful sorcerers in my life, but Kant had the talent more than others I've known. I don't think I've even heard of anyone who can do so much of the ... things he could do.

"I don't believe there are any elementals in Dinkard and probably not anywhere."

"You don't believe in elementals?" Lest asked.

"Not really," Z said. "I've heard all kinds of stories, but it's always someone's cousin's best friend's sister's former boyfriend who heard it from his aunt's best friend who heard it from the person who actually was in the same town with someone who saw the person who heard it from the one it happened to!

"Kirt droppings!"

Lest laughed heartily and agreed that was about the same kind of information he had so he didn't accept them as beings, but he thought they could be expressions of powers of some sort.

"I think everything happens in patterns," Z suggested. "All elementals are is somebody's attempt to explain why there *are* patterns. The tides are high on the coast when the moon is directly overhead so people decide there's an elemental in the moon who calls the water. Selipe is, therefore, the water elemental and he lives in the moon. They don't explain why the tide's also high when the moon isn't in the sky at all."

"The moon does affect the tides," Lest argued. "The tide is highest when the moon is directly overhead and at one half the time until it's overhead again. All we have to do is discover *why*! People made up the explanation of an elemental who can call water because they couldn't think of anything else.

"A man named Fraghert has made studies of the night heavens. A world traveler by the name of Mikill was here recently and he had met Fraghert a few years past and mentioned his studies. I have some writings by him and read them again since. He can't find a logical-seeming reason behind certain movements in the firmament and I have put thought into it. Mikill did say that others have studied anomalies in the movements of several of the stars as well as the connections between Selipe and the tides."

"Kant studied that kind of thing," Z agreed. "He said the same thing that makes us stay on Gaerkt would make us stay on Selipe if we were there. It pulls the water here and Gaerkt pulls the water there. He was pretty smart. I guess he was right, but I don't even try to understand it. I'm of a more simple bent."

"He thought there is water on Selipe?" Lest asked.

"He claims the sun's a sphere, Selipe's a sphere and Gaerkt must, obviously, also be a sphere," Z said. "Selipe's another whole world!"

"We can see the sun and Selipe are round – but also that

Gaerkt is flat," Lest argued.

"No, it's not! We know for a fact that Gaerkt is round!" Z cried triumphantly. "We see it all but six nights per cycle of Selipe. Kant proved that so even I can understand it!"

"But *how*?!" Lest demanded.

"The sun goes around Gaerkt making a bright light, right?" Z asked.

"But...." Lest protested.

"Selipe goes around Gaerkt, but it doesn't make any light of its own. Kant proved that, too," Z stated.

"I tend to agree that Selipe doesn't make any light of its own," Lest agreed.

"Kant claimed he could show us exactly how it works with three balls, then he showed me," Z said. "Put one ball in the middle, which is Gaerkt, and one to either side of Gaerkt to be the sun and Selipe."

"I can picture that," Lest said.

"Both the sun and the moon are moving around Gaerkt, east to west," Z continued. "Selipe is moving faster than the sun. A drip-timer shows it's moving around Gaerkt almost a whole period faster than the sun."

"I've seen models that would indicate that," Lest said. "The time is exact for both the sun and Selipe. Selipe goes around faster than the sun. This is something all sorcerers know and all people who think about it know. There is nothing in that to say Gaerkt is round!"

"Why does Selipe have phases?" Z asked.

"Why?" Lest returned after a moment's thought.

"Let me hold up this plate," Z declared. "It represents Selipe. The fire in the grate gives us light so it represents the sun. I move my hand between the fire and the plate. It casts a shadow on the plate ... see?"

"So it does, but.... I think I see what you.... I see!" Lest cried. "The shape of the shadow is the shape of your hand.

The shape of the shadow on Selipe is a circle so Gaerkt is a circle because the shadow is that of Gaerkt! It *has* to be! It was most wise of Kant to figure that out! Amazing! It was always so plain, yet no one knew it until now!"

"Actually it was the same process used by the ancient Babylonians, Egyptians and Mayans to reach the same conclusion thousands of years before Colombus, who proved the world was flat!" Z said.

"What?" Lest asked.

"It's an old legend in Dinkard," Z answered quickly. "It was about a hero who had set out to prove Gaerkt was round, but what he did would have proved it actually was flat – even though people accepted that it was round – because of what he did."

"I don't...?" Lest said.

"The hero set out to reach a place called India," Z said. "He went on the sea and what would have been over the edge if there had been an edge and he arrived at a place called Puerto Rico. His theory was that he would reach *India*, thus would prove the world was round. He *never* reached India. According to his own theory the world was *not* round! People in Dinkard say to this day that he proved the world to be round, which he did NOT!"

"I see," Lest said. "An interesting fable that tells much of how people think. Should such a trip be undertaken and should such a result befall people *would* say the world had been proved round. It's the same thing about the elementals. I feel this fable was why Kant decided to study the shape of Gaerkt?"

"The fable was one part of his research," Z agreed. "It was obvious to him the first time he considered the motions of the sun and Selipe that the phase was Gaerkt's shadow and that it was obvious that Gaerkt had to be round.

"He theorized that all large bodies – and he says the stars

are other worlds – will be spheres. He died without discovering why."

"It would have to do with the fact the sphere is the per-fect geometric shape," Lest said. "It is the most efficient of all shapes. Nature is always efficient. Sorcery studies these things. It is why I have decided to study sorcery. I have always had a compelling desire to learn."

"I don't have the mind for such deep things," Z insisted. "I'm only a guard from another place who wants a job. Luckily, I found one."

"I think you have lost a very great treasure when the golems left you," Lest said. "There is much to learn from such magical beings."

"Oh, not to worry. They've left me several times before," Z said offhandedly, taking a large drought of the beer. "They find amusement with someone else for a few days, then return. They become bored very quickly and are much used to travel. Once they know every room and hall in the castle they'll decide to come back to me."

"You've never tried to learn how they work?" Lest asked.

"I don't delve into magic," Z replied. "I don't have that kind of power. The only great thing I see about those golems is that they continue to work after Kant's dead and gone. I don't think I've ever heard of magic that strong before. It says strange things about Kant."

"I cannot understand how it could be," Lest agreed. "I have the power about as much as anyone, but it depends solely on *me*! If I lose my concentration on an independent item such as those golems they become mere bronze. They take their power only from what I can project to them. There is a chilling conclusion to be drawn if that is true of all such powers."

"It bothers me, too," Z said. "I know Kant's dead because I was at his funeral pyre. I saw his body burn. I had the great honor of relating the memory. I set the flame, yet, as I have said, I do *not* know that he is dead. Those golems being active tell me he is *not*!

"I've heard the stories of those who say there's a spirit in some people that lives after they're gone, but I believe that no more than I believe in the elementals. It's nothing but a wish."

"It is a perplexing puzzle," Lest agreed. "Still I would much enjoy talking with those golems. I have practice. My wife!"

"You could go to the castle or wait until they decide to come back to cloud my days," Z said with his grin. "I suppose you could call them with some spell."

"I sense there is much great power around them," Lest said. "I feel it moving at times and know where they are. I doubt I could give them orders to appear."

"*No*body can give them orders!" Z warned. "They might enjoy speaking with a sorcerer. They've done that in other places, but you should be warned: They aren't very pleasant to be around. One of the heads, the one we call No, is as deeply obnoxious as anyone you might ever be unfortunate enough to meet.

"I suppose Yes is as obnoxious in its own way."

"It is two sides of Kant's personality cast into the heads," Lest replied. "I imagine Kant was much like the balance of the two."

"Another sorcerer said much the same thing and I've thought a lot on it," Z agreed. "Kant was very much like you. Smart and pleasant with a little bit of the cynic just below the surface. He was sometimes blindly trusting and others was suspicious of everyone and everything, but was mostly a rather normal sort of person. People tended to like him."

They talked almost an hour more, Lest insisting Z had an

introspective mind he denied and an intelligent way of viewing things if a somewhat fatalistic one – note the fact he took employment with the guard because that was what he knew while also knowing it was to the profit of no one that such a guard even existed. Z found Lest to be as intelligent as anyone he'd ever met anywhere.

The rest of the night was mostly quiet and normal. He wondered what the golems were learning in the castle – but he wasn't about to ask!

The golems spent the night investigating almost every centimeter of that castle. I still have no solid ideas. There is nothing obvious there to be found.

It was a bright morning with some light clouds gathering in the hills Z could see from his window. There was a slight chill to the air.

"King Fonz doesn't have some kind of crazy chapel secreted away where he worships some old elemental?" Z said. "The court sorcerer isn't plotting with the sorcerers from other cities? There aren't any aliens here to interfere?

"Too bad they don't have priests or cults. That's a little strange in a mammalian society at this stage isn't it? Not to have any kind of organized religion?"

Among mammals, yes. It's not unheard of, but it is a little out of the normal way of these kinds of things. A lot is out of the ordinary here on a level while most of it is very much the norm for an easy world.

"I like Lest. I think he's as smart as anyone I've met in a long time," Z went on. "I did a little test of his ability to analyze and he came through much better than most."

You babbled on about some old tale from Earth! I couldn't figure what the hells you were doing!

"I screwed up there," Z agreed. "I made it a tale of this world so Lest won't ever know. The important thing to me was how fast he reached the conclusion I hadn't stated yet. He knows the world's round."

*Worlds with large moons such as this one and Earth will demonstrate their shape almost daily. You said that. Lest was able to take the fact of your hand's shadow – with the thumb sticking up and waving around – and relate to the shadow on the moon. He *is* extremely intelligent. He's really a genius in this society.*

"I don't think King Fonz is really behind this thing," Z said. "I hope the golems can find who *is*! We have to know that."

He went downstairs to the dawnmeal, chatted with Gild and went to the courtyard at the castle where he was assigned a kirt – which he was expected to take care of completely – and some weapons. Captain Gyr tried to get him to use the smaller and lighter shields they were issued, but he refused, saying his training was with his personal shield and it would be totally stupid to try to change now.

His eight students were there and would go through all the motions he showed them. Their attitude was, "If I must, I must. Let's get it over with."

He went to Gyr's office at the noonbreak and said his students weren't suitable for the training.

"Ha! Welcome to the system!" Gyr responded with a dry grimace. "They're here because there's not any other employment to fit their abilities. They get paid a minimal living wage so they stay one centimeter inside the limits of what we'll have to accept from them. They're bored and they have no natural ability for this kind of thing and certainly no desire to learn it. The golems had that part right! The whole thing's pointless and we all know it!

"Don't you *ever* let anyone know I said that!"

"I won't," Z promised. "I need the wages for a time so it's all the same with me. I've always hated this kind of training myself, but it's what I know. The difference was that it was something you might need in Dinkard and they all know it'll never be needed here.

"Where *are* the golems?"

"They decided to look for King Fonz," Gyr answered. "They can match wits with him for a few hours, but I don't think they can bait him into anything like they can me. I suppose they'll come back when they get bored. He'll just look at them sort of funny and ignore them."

"Maybe they'll find someone who they can drive mad in the castle," Z said. "They're very good at *that*!

"Who was that sexy darkhaired girl who was watching us practice this morning? The one in the blue dress? She's some kind of beauty!"

"*That* is Judge Mako's daughter," Gyr said. "If you're stupid enough to respond to her rather obvious invitation don't ever do anything that might put you in court. You might find yourself moving large stones in the mountain fort!"

"The mountain fort?" Z asked.

"They're building a sort of castle/fort in the hills," Gyr replied. "It's something for the criminals to do, mostly. It's over ten kilometers away, there are constant guards and there are no girls closer than right here to attract you to their charms.

"Another pointless make-labor project. There are no less than nine people working on that place who took an interest in Luxe – that's her name – and later were brought before Judge Mako. Once told you're informed! Beware!"

"There's that kind of girl with that kind of father in about every place I've been," Z agreed. "She seemed very interested in me. Thanks for the warning."

"She's very interested in anyone who can be referred to as male," Gyr said. "It's too bad she's among the elite. She'd make a good dockworker's night station."

"We call them `sheports' around the docks in Dinkard," Z said. "Five credits the night with the itchy-scabbies thrown in free!"

They traded a few bawdy stories, then Z went back out to try to train his reluctant students. He decided to teach them a lot about their kirts first. He could claim (rightly) fighting from kirt back was only as efficient as the rider's skills. If they couldn't stay on the beast they sure as the snows couldn't *fight* from their backs!

In the afternoon he saw Lest sitting on a stone bench arguing with the golems so he went over to say his good fortunes.

–Well! If it isn't our insipid warrior! Did you manage to fall on your head more than ten times today?–

+Now, No! Be nice! Zho probably didn't fall off of the kirt more than twice all morning!

+I trust you are well, Zho? It certainly is a lovely day, isn't it? I was telling Lest here about the wonderful luck we've been having with the weather lately!+

–Ahhhh, stick it in your nose, Bugle Beak! It's been raining most of the damned morning and will probably pour barrels this afternoon! This gucky scum water screws up my finish! It's not good for another damned thing!–

+Now, No! Be nice! The rain makes the plants grow and the flowers bloom and washes everything to such a bright glow! A little polish and we're as good as new! You shouldn't be *quite* so critical of nature's little refreshing showers! You *are* a *mite* grumpy today. One should try to meet the little inconveniences of a normal life with realizations that the greater view is replete with many wonderful things that add to the better qualities of....+

–GAAAH! If you tell me to be nice one more time I'm gonna see if maybe those stones in the balustrade are harder than cast bronze, Nul Noggin! Sheesh! You could make a maggot puke! Just say the damned day isn't as bad as some we've lived through! We don't need a twenty four hour filibuster about the damned weather!–

"Make for a pleasant afternoon, don't they?" Z asked.

"Never dull," Lest agreed, returning Z's big grin. "About once every hour they say something intelligent.

"I'm assuming they'll say something intelligent within the hour. I haven't been here that long yet."

–WHAT THE..?! Sir Brilliant wants *us* to say something intelligent? Who would understand it?–

+Now, No. You have to admit we aren't acting exactly like the wisest of people. If you'd be a *lit*tle bit more positive in your dour demeanor perhaps the day would go faster and the....+

–*Wise*?! Look, Sand for Brains! If he ain't even gonna understand intelligent he sure ain't gonna recognize wise – and we ain't people in case you haven't noticed. We're golems! You ain't wise or intelligent! You're lucky if you make it as high as moronic!–

"I'll leave you to your misery," Z said. "You golems try to leave some small part of his sanity intact. I enjoy talking with him of an evening."

+Have a nice day, Zho! I'll take your sage advice and attempt to conduct myself in more of a proper manner and I'll also try to cajole No into acting with a *tiny* bit more decorum. I can see how one might get the impression that we both are....+

–Nice day? You'll *cajole* me? It's raining harder and you couldn't cajole a rodent into its own burrow, Brass Ass!–

Lest chuckled and Z shook his head and waved as he walked away. Yes was saying, +No! Be a little considerate of others' feelings! You tend to be just a *teensy* bit coarse at times and I wish you'd think before you make some of your remarks. Smile and the town smiles with you. Frown and....+

–AHHHHHHHHH! SHUT UP!"–

"When you shoot the arrow you have to release the reins and rise off the saddle," Z instructed. "You leave your knees a bit flexible to counter the rise and fall of the kirt. If you can't train yourself to do that simple thing you can't ever hope to hit a target from the moving kirt. All this is pointless unless your kirt knows how to move at the proper time so the first thing we'll do is train your kirts to move straight ahead at a steady pace when you give the command and drop the reins.

"You see this little knob I screwed onto the front of the saddle? I call it a saddlehorn.

"You have to be able to drop the reins so they catch behind the horn. If they fall to the side you can't regain control of the mount quickly enough when you fire the arrow and you'll end up being the one who's shot.

"You'll each have to make your own saddlehorn and attach it. I made mine so it breaks free fairly easily, but some in Dinkard made them a part of the saddle that won't come off. If your mount drops forward in a hole and you slide, think about what can happen if that thing won't come loose easily – and do what you want about attaching it more permanently or so it can break away.

"Once you've fired the arrow you sit back into the saddle, reach across your shoulder into the quiver in a steady sweeping motion like this, then rise again as you fit the bowstring.

"You can't do any of it until your kirt is trained to keep moving at a steady pace and in a straight line with only short vocal commands so we'll concentrate on training the kirts now and us later.

"We'll first learn to mount as a unit. Everyone is to make the same movement at the same time in this practice. I want you to watch me and listen to my commands. I'll mount and ride to the curve of the outroad, then come back.

"This will seem silly to most of you. Getting on a kirt and riding straight ahead, then turning around and coming back is something you all know.

"I'll wager not one of you will do it right the first time!

"Any takers?"

They snickered and shrugged, but no one bet. He asked why.

"Because you make the rules so you can say we were wrong no matter what we do," one of them answered. "We've all been caught in that one! It's how the guard works. The top officer will give an order, it's stupid, and you get blamed because it was wrong."

"That's not how I operate," Z replied. "Watch me and learn something. I will say only that I'm righthanded."

He stood by the kirt, said "Foot!" loudly, placed his foot in the stirrup, then said "Mount!" and swung fluidly up and into the saddle. He said, "Reins!" and picked them up with his left hand. He then called "Ahead!" and started the mount forward at a steady pace, went to the curve and returned.

He told them to get to their mounts.

Two of them immediately mounted.

He shook his head and called, "Foot!" The others placed their feet in the stirrups with knowing grins, determined that they wouldn't get ahead of themselves.

"Mount!" They swung into the saddles passably well. Three of them also picked up the reins immediately, realized they'd messed it up and one dropped the reins again.

"Backwards!" Z yelled and another picked up the reins. Two started riding forward, stopped and came back. The others started making remarks and they all decided to have some fun with it.

"Reins!" Z yelled and all who weren't already holding the reins picked them up – in their left hands.

"Ahead!" They all rode to the curve and back where Z called to dismount.

"Every one of you screwed up – and not because I'm making anything up," he said. "Before you say it, you know you messed up except for Yan, who did everything exactly as I showed you, but he also screwed up because I decided to let you think some things out for yourselves.

"Maybe one or two of the rest of you did the same thing. Someone tell me what I mean."

"I think probably it has to do with your telling us that you were righthanded," Wil said after a minute. "You told us you were righthanded and you picked up the reins with your left. Yan picked up the reins with his left hand, too, but he's lefthanded. I don't see what difference it makes, but that's it isn't it?"

"Yes. That's it exactly!" Z agreed with a grin. "You have to get the kirt accustomed to responding to the reins from the hand you don't need to remove the bow and arrow. It must not become confused by you normally using one hand and then suddenly shifting when there's the most need for it to respond in a fixed pattern. If you do that *you* break the pattern. It's not the fault of the kirt."

"So we would have every one lost if we'd bet," Tor said. "And we all have to say you were true when you said we'd be able to see it wasn't made up. Maybe we *will* learn something from you!"

"You'll see how important this is later, but we're going to make twelve trips between here and that curve. By the last one I hope we'll have it down to perfection," Z said. "Remember which hand to use. That will be important later

– more than you can know.

"Ready! Foot!"

They did the simple exercise the rest of the afternoon. The last three runs were as close to perfect as he could hope. He was beginning to get the respect of the men and was learning respect for them in turn. They were more at ease with one another. In the morning he would train them to do the same thing, but in a set formation. He'd have to work that formation out so no archer would be in the way of any other, but that would be simple enough. He would figure a triangular sector for each. The lesson would have to be that no one could fire outside of his triangle unless there was no alternative. Always understand that a given situation might alter the rules, but only to a fixed degree.

Luxe was hanging around the stables as he took the kirt in to feed and brush it, but he ignored her. Lest and a large woman he introduced as his wife, Marla, and a somewhat suspicious and sour older man were passing through. They stopped for introductions. Z met Judge Mako. He wasn't impressed.

"You have the kirts trained to move in a straight line after you drop the reins and to not change pace unless you command them to," Z reviewed three days later. "You know the motion of dropping the reins and rising so your knees act as level riding supports, flexing down as the kirt rises then straightening to compensate as it drops under you.

"That will take a lot of tedious work, but you can get so your shoulders move at the same level as you go along.

"You've been told about the firing triangle pattern to concentrate on, but not why because that will be obvious to anyone with half a brain. It's only mentioned now because it shows the absolute necessity of the pattern of the formation you ride in. We're practicing all this at a slow trot until it becomes a second nature to you and to your kirt, then we'll speed it up and slow it down so you can do the same at almost any speed. You will have to always keep to formation and the kirts will have to handle a good part of that with a verbal command. You call 'formation' to them and they keep the same pace and distance of the lead rider, who will be whoever is in front on the left side. You've all ridden that position.

"This morning we'll give the kirts a rest while we practice pulling the bow and placing the first arrow. You might think it would be best to practice that on kirt back, but I guarantee you that's not the case. I think you've learned that I know how to teach these things by now.

"We're going to do the same movement until you hate my lousy stinking ass! I think you've learned how valuable that kind of practice is by now, too.

"Believe me, if you ever need any of this stuff you'll love my stinking lousy ass for being such a driver.

"You will first practice the movement sitting astride these

logs I've put on these braces. It isn't as easy as it looks and I don't want you hurting either yourselves or your kirts."

He climbed atop one of the logs, hung his shield off to the left side and placed the bow in its normal carrying position across one shoulder. He was exaggerating every movement. They'd learned it was much easier on them if they got things right the first time. It saved them hours of tedious drill.

"You are riding along on patrol and the order is given to attack," he lectured as he made each described motion. "You drop the reins across the saddlehorn, say `Steady charge! Formation!' to your kirt, reach up like this to grasp the bow just above the quiver with your left hand – if you're righthanded.

"As you raise yourself to attack position, knees bent beside the saddle with your weight on the stirrups, grab an arrow at the same time, sweep the bow outward, bringing up the other hand to take the base of the arrow and place it on the string and hold it in place, moving the other hand outward with the bow.

"Flatten the bow like this and keep your left arm rigid with the thumb bent a little upward. It guides the arrow into proper alignment. You are automatically ready to fire in one smooth motion. It must be fluid and automatic.

"Swing the bow around and downward and release as you pass the target point. *Don't* try to draw directly on the point on a moving mount. Start a few centimeters high on a far target and more on a close target, which seems backward until you think on it and let fly as you pass the sight point.

"I'll do it in real speed now instead of so slow."

He went through the motion smoothly and quickly, letting the arrow fly to strike the target thirty meters away in the blue center spot. He reached back in a fluid motion to flip another arrow into place on the string. He had practiced this a bit when there was no one about, but it was mostly from the crystal.

"You'll learn to do this riding at any speed."

–That was as sloppy as you've ever done it, Gong Face!–
No greeted as the floater came from the castle to hover a
meter over Z's head. –If you're that slow in Dinkard you're
as good as dead vulture food!–

+Now, No! You know perfectly well Zho hasn't been able
to practice for more than a year. You can't expect perfection
this quickly.+

–I don't expect perfection, Bonghead! I *do* expect a little
less *im*perfection! Your mind – such as it is – has more
stupid twists than a loopserpent in heat!–

"I'd hoped you two had found someone else to try to drive
insane at the castle," Z replied. "Not enough of a
challenge?"

+I have to report the bunch of them seem a little less than
wholly sane already. They have every mental quality except
logic, note that you are training useless warriors.

+No can sometimes be a tiny *mite* irritating and they didn't
seem to appreciate the excellent advice I was giving them
about the economy. They certainly could put proper advice
to use! There are any number of incentives and drivers that
could be inserted into the financial....+

–Ahhh, stick it in your nose, Snake Snoot! If your
economic advice was any damned good you wouldn't be
such a pain in the neck! You might want to explain why
with all your great economic expertise you ain't rich! You
might explain why you're giving economic instructions,
such as they are, to kirtsmen!

–What the nine hells do they care, Waffle Brain?–

"I'm trying to teach these men something about riding and
shooting," Z said. "Leave us alone. Go bother some-one
else."

–Them as can't do, teach! – not to mention there ain't no

reason to teach this crap here anyhow, Snap Snoot! Did that ever occur to you or are you like the rest of these fribblesloths? Just take the money and don't cloudy the damned skies! That captain has more brains than you about that point!–

+It gives them something to do. If one must pass the time it's at least nice to know they can enjoy the beautiful scenery and the brightness of this beautiful day outdoors!

+As I said to Lest only the other day, the weather here is delightful! There is the hint of coolness of autumn in the air and the cool afternoon showers are so refreshing! Soon the snows will come and it won't be so pleasant so we should all enjoy it while it's here! The sun dapples its myriad hues on the sparkling meadow as....+

–GHEEE! Look, Tin Tongue, I'm getting bored with this stupid sameness all the time! These rocktoads don't ever *do* anything!

–Maybe we should go find Lest. He's usually able to make an intelligent reply to questions if none of these other are! One question in five anyhow. One in ten?–

"Bye!" Z said.

+We'll see you later at the inn, Zho. No is a *little* bit grumpy today. I've tried to tell him to relax and enjoy the *won*derful play of merry zephyrs teasing the tips of the lithe undulating green grasses that coat the....+

–AHHHHH, SHUT THE GORK UP!–

They flew away. The trainees were laughing heartily. Z shook his head and went on with the lesson.

Viz tried it first, caught the edge of his bow against the log and fell off into the grey dust. Everyone was laughing at the golems already and that put them in a good mood that would last all day.

The golems were going to be back at the inn so either they found what they were after at the castle – or they didn't.

I've been busy so the golems are mostly on their own. The computer records everything and is programmed with what to look for. I'll review it now.... Hmmm-ummm. Nothing too very surprising, unexpected or interesting. Lest is intelligent and is really enjoying the golems. He can come up with some of those things you call zingers against No, who respects him for it at the same time it gets angry.

"In other words they didn't learn anything," Z agreed. "I didn't think they did or they wouldn't have said they would be back here.

"I wonder if that Luxe girl knows anything. She might if she's slept with the right people."

*No doubt you'll discover the best way to learn about that is to sleep with her yourself. *You* at least will remain entirely predictable that way!*

Z grinned and cleaned up, then went down to the inn to have a hot meal. Captain Gyr decided it would be better if he stayed there and the king paid for his room and board. Lest was sitting at a side table with the golems hovering overhead arguing with him about something. He seemed greatly amused.

"Are you still reasonably sane?" Z greeted.

"I sometimes find a great deal of wisdom in the things Yes and No say," Lest replied. "It's a matter of selecting what they say and looking at it from a new angle. Like with Marla.

"I see you've managed to actually teach the king's guards something new. Congratulations! I would have called it a probably futile experiment had I not been a direct witness.

"One cannot teach another a thing that other refuses to learn. It is an exercise in futility."

"I find they will quickly learn whatever they're interested in learning – so I try to make it interesting," Z said. "They like kirtback riding and that's part of what they should know so concentration on those skills keeps them trying to learn. I've also used a little subterfuge by saying little things to make them want to compete with each other. I still have no idea why they're being taught these things. There's no use for any of the warrior skills here. It seems to be nothing more than waste.

"I'm not complaining! It's employment that's easy and that pays well enough."

"If you ever learn anything let me know," Lest replied. "It's a puzzle, but I don't see any danger in it – though the golems say the danger's there and I could see it if I 'could think past my next meal,' as No puts it."

–Smoke Brain can't see what he's doing so he goes right on training those idiots! Maybe it's about time to point out the obvious to you!–

"Do that!" Z replied quickly to forestall Yes from saying anything.

–Would you train anybody for a long time and with a lot of expense if you don't plan to use them for anything?–

"You're saying the fact King Fonz is training them means he'll have to use them?" Lest asked. "Marla says that."

–Yay-yo! Give that man a sweetcake! Great elementals of Gaerkt! He can actually see what's so obvious!–

+Now, No! There's no *place* to use them here and nothing to use them *for*! Your point is valid in certain circumstances, but is without basis here. If you wouldn't be so negative all the time you might see the king is simply supplying gainful employment to people. They have so many around they have to find *some*thing for them to do!

+If you would simply try to look a *lit*tle bit on the positive side of things....+

–AAAHHHHH, stick it in your stupid ear, Slugbreath! 'Simply' is the way you look at everything because you're simple!–

The antics of the golems was now getting giggles from some of the patrons.

"I'll agree there's more employment available than it would seem," Lest said. "Much of what is available here requires little or no special talent or knowledge. I see falsity in the ideas being put forward that every job takes special training."

"You can convince people of anything," Z agreed. "I'll never understand it, but I've seen that sort of idea manipulation in a lot of places."

–It's because you Midge Minds will believe anything that'd make you think you're special yourself! This place here has a sign asking for a trained worker to help run the inn!

–We can ignore that nobody's coming from anywhere else to have the training – except for us, and our training is in other areas.

–Sit at the damned desk and tell people you have a room or you don't and sweep out the rooms every few days! Yeah! That takes all kinds of training! Maybe Bone Beam here can take a few years off from training useless war-riors to train useless innkeepers! Even *you* two could do that with a little practice.–

+I hate it when I have to agree with you. I purely hate it!+

–You don't hate it half as much as I do when I have to agree with *you*, Sugar Brain!–

"I hate it most of all whenever I have to agree with *both* of you!" Z threw in. "That was one of the things I saw right at the first when I was getting my room. Anyone can do that work, but Gild's convinced it takes specialized training. I wondered why she would believe that, but it seems to be the way all of the people here think."

They discussed it, slowly bringing Lest around to question whether it was reasonable to go to the expense and trouble of training warriors for no purpose. Z finally left to go to the public pub near the castle where his students often went in the evenings. Luxe would be there he was sure.

She was.

What did you learn from sleeping with that silly self-absorbed nymphomaniac?

"Not much this soon," Z replied. "It was an interesting night. She really can't control herself with sex."

It was another bright morning with a distinct chill in the air. Maita predicted a fast-moving cold front would be arriving before dawn followed by another stronger front the following night. Temperatures would drop to or below the freezing point of water.

–*She* can't control *her*self?!– No cried from the top of the massive dresser-cabinet. –I got some news for you, Vulture Breath! You weren't exactly what I'd call reserved! You mammals sure are noisy with that sex stuff!–

"Have you been there all night?!" Z demanded.

–Certainly! You'd prefer we stayed on the roof in this freezing cold? What the hells do we care what you do?–

+Now, No! You know how inhibited he is! For years he's been trying to overcome his silly taboos. We must try to understand the feelings of other and should restrain our remarks.

+You do tend to be a *lit*tle bit loudish when you're doing things like that, Zho. Just a *mite* more decorum might possibly be in order, but I can't understand the emotional imperatives that are released when you are involved in those intimate....+

–*Decorum*!? Look, Dung Dome! Those organic types are always loud and vulgar when they're in bed together! Sheesh!–

I assume from that reply you feel you'll have to sleep with her at least a few more times before you can learn anything of any real significance?

"Maybe once more," Z said with a smirk. "These things take time and patience. We aren't, as you've said, in any hurry here so I'll take my time to be sure I don't miss anything.

"I've decided to start a competition among my students to challenge all others to a contest of skills I'm teaching them. I can discover what they know and learn if there's something from outside of this place influencing this mess."

You think aliens? There's no evidence of it. As to your big sacrifice and willingness to take your time with Luxe, picture the well-known salute with the middle finger extended and the others in a fist.

"I don't know what I think," Z replied slowly, grinning. "It could be anything. Remember how Tab and Kit found that intelligent fungus. We would never have believed there could be such a thing and look how well those Tlessarian brains were able to infiltrate those societies with androids.

"This is military, which immediately brings to mind those Tlessarian robots. Still, it's more subtle than any of that so it might be a local aberration. I don't know what to think and I can't find who – or what's – behind it. The Tlessarian brain couldn't be anywhere near here. It doesn't have FTL ships."

I can detect minor power fluctuations all over the world, but they're psy-driven from the sorcerers. I can't understand why they haven't called any demons from other planes so I might be gone for a few hours to see what's there at this nexus. Maybe there isn't anything. Remember how we found Kurk!

"Well, we have a robotic brain, an intelligence that evolved separately here, an otherplanal being interfering and a purely local phenomenon," Z answered. "The possibilities are ... interesting. Whatever it is it's different!"

–We also have rain on the brain! The whole thing's going

to be based on a stupid damned psychological point! I just know it! I can always feel these things and I just *know* it! Ten boring years on this primitive world among a bunch of savages and it's some kind of a psychological point you can't do anything about anyhow!–

+Again, I'm embarrassed to have to agree with No. This is too slow and too disorganized to be anything else. I can feel it also. There is nothing directing this muddle from outside simply because it IS such a muddle. A directing would be to a plan that would eventuate into a societal driver mechanism to instill....+

–GAK! Here we go again! Maybe after Bilge Head sleeps with Frump Rump a few more times he'll be able to figure it out!– No said, for once, brightly.

+It's such a nice day today! It's got that *lit*tle touch of autumn in the air that so invigorates one, don't you think? Maybe we should go on a picnic! The warm sunshine is dappling its merry spotlights on the soft green of the....+

–DAPPLING its SPOTLIGHTS?! GHAAAAH! It's going to get colder than interspace tomorrow! You call that a little touch of autumn?! If you had any sense I don't think I could stand it!

–We're bronze, in case it's slipped you tiny little mind, Blab Tab! We don't *eat* picnic crap!–

+Now, No! Be nice! It's going to be lovely today so we'll wait until tomorrow to fret about inclement weather! We can't do anything about it so let's just enjoy the good and put the bad aside until such time as....+

"AHHHH, SHUT THE HELLS UP!" Z yelled.

+What?!+ Yes was shocked.

–Say what?!–

What!?

"Hah! Got you!" Z cried, picking up the shield and heading for the door. "I got to No's line before he could!"

–I'll get you for that, Barge Ass!– There was a little chuckle under the words.

+Really, Zho! You'll disturb the other patrons of the inn! I thought you had promised to keep *us* quiet, now you make all that noise yourself! You really must try to control your emotions a bit more. We were already remarking about your proclivity to become noisy with the sex things. You shouldn't extend that into other situations, though I will admit the provocation was a bit different this time. You teach patience and....+

–AAAAH! Just say to tone it down, Blither Puss!–

The floater came to hover over his head and make remarks as they went down the stairs to dawnmeal.

It was going to be an interesting day.

Trying, but interesting.

"What we're going to do today is ride the kirts from back by the wall, rise into attack position as we pass the white pole, shoot at the target, return to normal riding position and rein up at the red pole," Z said. "I'll ride through the drill first. We'll move at slow trot, one at the time.

"Line up in the order we've practiced. I'll make my ride, then go to the target area to mark your shots and retrieve the arrows.

"This is the hardest part to get right. We can ride and fire and all that, but we also have to be able to hit the target or it's all for nothing. As the old saying in Dinkard goes, it's irrelevant who shoots first if he doesn't hit anything."

He mounted his kirt, rode out, fired at the target getting almost dead center of the circle, then rode around to dismount a few meters from the target. He waved for the first rider to come through the drill. It had become a bit of a point of pride to be able to do the things Z demanded of them on the first try and they knew they were going to have to do this drill so they'd been practicing when he wasn't around. All of them hit the target if not very close to the center.

"Very good!" Z complimented them when they'd all made their runs. "I think you're actually going to be able to make decent bowriders!

"I've been thinking. We know perfectly well there's no real purpose for any of this so why not design our own skill games around the drills? Maybe we could hold a competition and have prizes. We could invite anyone to join the games so it would keep us sharp and alert!"

There was some murmured agreement. It would take away from the stale tedium of the constant practice drills.

"We'll get together to design a contest course later," Z continued. "I want you to practice this until you can hit within the center circle with every shot. Once you've accomplished that we can work on riding in groups. We have to find the pattern that'll work best with what we have."

"Do we need set patterns for that?" Viz asked. "I'd think patterns would be a problem in a battle because the enemy would know where everyone is."

"That's very observant, but we move in a patterned manner on patrols and so forth," Z agreed. "We all realize there's never going to be any use of this unit in any battles, so we can make it a parade unit, but we can't let Captain Gyr and his superiors know we're doing that if you get the way the stream flows."

It was a joke among them that they were being trained in a totally useless job so they would play along. It was mostly fun to them by that point and they were actually becoming highly skilled kirt riders. There was some pride in that. A parade would show off their personal skills and a competition would do the same.

"Maybe we could make small wagers on the compe-titions," Yan said. "People could bet like they do with the regular kirt races and jumps and wrestling!"

"Yeah!" Tor agreed. "We could even have a wagering stand. Get a little business venture of our own started."

"I'd agree to that under one condition and *only* under one condition," Z said. "There will be *no* cheating – in any form. The temptation to change the outcome of a compe-tition where there's a lot of wagering on one contestant and little on another will be great. We must ensure there will *never* be that stigma placed on our games!"

These people were basically honest and were easy to stir up by any suggestion of impropriety so they started discussing how to keep the games honest. Z said for them to think about it while they practiced the drills. The fact that they were planning a strong competition that could profit them directly made them eager to get as good at the drills as possible. The rest of the day was very easy for Z.

"I think the best way is to make it known that any cheating and the cheater's name will be posted publicly," Wil suggested. "That will make sure nobody cheats!"

"We can make minor infractions a matter of public posting of names and major ones a serious matter of being expelled from any of the future competitions for all time," Z agreed. "I'll bet the king's court will be glad to pass sentence on the worst things and can send the criminals to the hill fort for a few days!"

"*That* will do it!" Tor said. "We can be sure no one'll want to join Mako's troops there!"

They were at the inn to discuss the planned games – or to plan them, anyhow. The whole day had been spent with the training unit discussing it among themselves and with planning the different things to be included.

"We can have teams of no more than four competitors so our eight riders can make two teams," Z suggested. "We can hold competitions with some of the things I'm going to be teaching you soon. I think we should start learning something about other ways the kirts can be used in these games. We can get into games that take a lot more skill and courage than these drills.

"Kirts are good at jumping over things. We can put some logs on tripods and teach the kirts to jump the thing with us firing at the top of the jump. That's a skill I can teach you, but you can make your own estimates of how many not in our little group could hope to even try such a feat."

–These dolts will kill themselves trying that kind of thing, Bulge Butt!– No snapped from the golem's position hovering above the table. –I'd wager if you had any logic you'd be dangerous! You think a thing halfway through on your best days!–

The golems threw in such snide quips now and again, but were mostly not being so obnoxious as usual.

"That's the excitement!" Wil cried. "It adds some danger to the games! It will also show people how our training is for something besides just a way to make a living!"

+That doesn't make any sense, Wil. It's still for nothing, but life is made interesting and even as you've so very aptly noticed, exciting, by such light diversions. To supply theater and art to a basically useless venture has great value in itself. It is art that makes life worth the living. Without it a drabness and monotony would soon find its way into the psyche of each of....+

–How the nine hells would you know anything about living, you bronze excuse for a brass door holder!? You could make a casketworm puke! What's this crap about art? *You* think sandworm tracks are art!–

That was to inform Z he'd said enough for the time. If he

kept the ideas at the right intensity it would work. Push too fast and interest would die. Too slow and it wouldn't begin. Maita was directing the golems for that.

Luxe was sitting across the inn giving him meaningful looks every time he glanced her way so he soon broke up the meeting and went to his room. She followed before long. The golems quietly informed him that there was someone watching her before she appeared at his door.

He made another little plan, then.

What did you learn from sleeping with that overblown nymphomaniac?

"Other than the fact she thinks her father's the slimiest sleazy rockslug who ever wandered into the king's court, nothing," Z replied as he climbed out of bed. Luxe had left only minutes before. "I think she sort of resents that her father will try to put everyone who even looks at po' widdle ol' innercent her in the hill fort on any pretext he can find. I'll have to be careful to stay out of trouble for a little longer, then I can do something to make him send me there."

You want to go to the hill fort? Why?

"To see what's so important they would build the place at all and maybe to see who's actually in charge here," Z replied. "I'm going to have to do something to force a reaction from someone. Nobody ever gives any orders because nothing ever happens. I can't know who's actually the boss until they give someone an order. All I'm personally sure of is that it's *not* King Fonz!

"Where are the golems this morning?"

They decided to tag along with your student troops to keep the ideas of the festival going. You might force your transfer orders because of that when the big bosses find out about it. You're diverting attention away from the violence idea and back toward playing games, which is subverting whatever they're planning. We'll have to see if they can do anything to reverse it now. It will definitely, as you've so colorfully put it, cramp their style.

"I don't think they can, which is why I started it," Z said. "If the idea strays away from their objective these people will refuse to change so they'll have to come up with some new plan. I have the added little charm that they can't start talking much against the games without people getting resentful and asking why there could be anything wrong with a little competition. I'm also going to try to push the idea that these little competitions will cause the troops to sharpen their skills far beyond what they would be able to do without the incentives.

"The thing I have to concentrate on is seeing that all their arguments are answered before they're made. I'll do my best to start building a lot of frustration into it for the bosses. I'll bring up new things with the most wide-eyed innocence you ever saw.

"'Whah, Kind Sir! Ah thought what y'all has done hired me foah is tah train these heah *fine* young sohdjer boys how they can do somethin' con-struh-uc-tive! Whah, now wasn't it *yoah verah-ry own* con-ten-she-un that they was jist bein' given this heah job so as to keep them off'n the welfare rolls from the ve-ah-ry first? Did Ah somehow *mis*understand what you-all done hired me foah, heah?'"

That kind of act will end you up in the hill fort because they won't know what else to do with you! It should be perfectly clear who causes your arrest. Maybe we'll be able to use this better than anything else. It's a chance to find out what we've said from the first we had to know: who's in charge of this crap with a military?

"Something has to work right sooner or later," Z agreed. "We haven't accomplished a single thing so far – that we came here for, but we have done some positive things, I think. I think we've managed to do a lot with Lest and with the directions we're turning this stupid warmonger mentality. I think we've already changed this society for the better.

"I believe I've worked out a riding pattern that will seem very logical to anyone who doesn't know much about military attack strategies – and no one here does. One thing we *do* know here is that they don't have the least conception about how to train warriors. It's never been a part of anything here before."

We have to see it doesn't become part of anything.

Z went downstairs to the dawnmeal, then out to his training area to find his troops in very high spirits. The golems were acting like they always did and the troops were taking it in good humor and were even returning some of No's caustic remarks. Everything was light and easy as they practiced the rides and firing at the targets. Most shots were striking within the major circle and some were finding their way into the center circle with good regularity.

After the noonmeal/rest break Z suggested a patterned group ride approach and set the targets, four for each group, at various distances. He took them to his planning table to instruct them when a man came to join them.

"I am King's Judge Mako," he introduced himself. "I find some interest in these preparations and would greatly appreciate some candid explanations of what you're doing and why."

The troops became immediately exceedingly nervous. They'd seen Luxe hanging around the inn and knew she'd been to Z's room.

"I'm called Zho," Z said, then introduced the remainder of his unit. "I imagine there's no breach of confidence to telling the King's Judge what we're learning and why so you might find some interest in joining this planning session to learn for yourself how efficiently these things can be done.

"You will realize how much we've learned already and how skilled we're becoming. (He winked at the troops sitting across from him and Mako at the table.) We take pride in doing a thing right for the honor of our king.

"The first run will be the standard ridethrough and shot, riding at the medium to fast pace to give you the feel of the course. Then I want Yan to ride to the right and in front of the patterned charge drill with Wil next and to his left. Wil will ride one kirt-length behind Yan. Tor will follow immediately behind on the right. Viz will be immediately behind Wil.

"Yan is lefthanded, as is Tor. Your normal inclination is to, therefore, fire your arrows to the right. Righthanded Wil and Viz have a natural tendency to fire toward their left so no one fires across their fellow riders' paths.

"That is very important! *Never* fire across the path of your fellows!

"The second group will be Rik and Lab on the right and Obe and Vik on the left.

"I'll ride among you for the first ridethrough. You'll go through the motions on the group ride, but you won't release the arrows. It will be a one-shot ride this first time to give you the feel of the course, then we'll stagger the targets and let you make two or three shots across the course.

"Any questions?"

They made sure everyone knew his position at all times, then Z rode the course fast, alone, putting an arrow almost perfectly into the blue center. That ride stimulated the others into trying to best him and the single run was a truly great success. Mako was amazed at both the speed and accuracy they attained.

They made the team ridethroughs, Z explained every least

little slip they'd made and they rode through it at a slow trot to fire the first round. It was only a little bit better than he'd hoped, but completely flabbergasted Mako, who was standing next to Z near the targets.

"You do not fear standing so close to where they're going to shoot?" Mako asked.

"Not anymore," Z answered. "They're trained for this. The single rides are so well-executed now that no one has missed a target in four days. They'll adjust to the patterned patrol unit concept very quickly and I'll venture a wager not one will miss the target entirely by the third ride. They're slowly coming around to where they'll become a very efficient unit. They have some basic skills to learn yet, but the knowledge of them – which would be dan-gerously premature at this time – will strike terror into any enemy."

"You said they'll make several shots on later rides?" Mako asked. "Do you extend the ride for that?"

"Rik! Tor! Set the targets for a fast ridethrough, single!" Z called. "This is a demonstration to show what I'll expect from everyone when the training's finished, so make it difficult. You know the projections so let's show Judge Mako we've wasted not one minute of the time the king's been paying us to learn!"

He mounted his kirt and waited. This was a difficult ride even for him. The crystal had only the few limitations of the person the skill was recorded from, plus what he had been able to add through practice. He wanted to be impressive while remaining well within safety factors.

The four in his elite team placed the staggered targets – and stood close beside them! He didn't really plan for that, but couldn't back down now.

Z was sweating a little bit as he spurred the mount forward at a medium running speed. He whipped off the bow and fired, slung back another arrow and fired, then another, then another. He ended the course run and raced back through from the reverse direction, firing four more times. His confidence was very high on the reverse run-through. He'd held the kirt back just enough! Every one of the eight shots was within the center circle, though none was dead center. Mako was unbelieving as was Marla, Lest's wife, who had come to join them as he started the run.

"I've never seen such kirtmanship or such marksmanship with the bow!" Marla exclaimed. "You centered *every single arrow*!

"Amazing! I would have said it couldn't be done!"

"You have to be able to do that if you're to be effective as a force," Z replied. "I admit to a bit of an attack of nerves on that ride because I'm still training the unit and wasn't quite prepared to demonstrate even this small part of the training. If you ask the men they'll tell you I'm generally far more accurate than that. I didn't center any of the shafts. I merely got within the bounds of the center circle. That is *not* good enough to pass my own standards!

"I think you'll admit that anyone planning to move against Castiel who had heard of this unit when each is trained to do *better* than my poor demonstration ride will decide to travel elsewhere!"

"I had reports that you were quite a good teacher, but I had no idea!" Mako said. "This is amazing! It's positively amazing!"

"Do you mean to tell us there are other arts that you're teaching the troops? Did I understand you correctly? This is not all of it?" Marla asked.

"If this was all they could do they would be too limited to be of any real use because they'd have to wait for the enemy to move according to our plans, but it serves to show that I can teach!" Z replied proudly. "I have a lot of things to teach these men! I'm rather surprised at how very *little* they know of these things!"

"Amazing! Positively amazing! This kind of special troop training will make us absolutely invincible!" Mako cried. "*No* one could hope to withstand such an attack! *No* one!

"Amazing! "I need not say how very deeply impressed I am with this practice!

"Amazing!"

"I'm glad you approve," Z said. "I have to make a few minor adjustments in the sloppy way they rode that last runthrough, but I suppose they'd naturally be as nervous as I am when they have the King's Judge watching the maneuvers."

"I certainly don't wish to cause any problems with this amazing group!" Mako exclaimed. "Let me say I am proud and most impressed with you all! Perhaps Zho found something sloppy, as he said about your runthrough, but I will yet insist I found it amazing! Positively amazing!

"I will leave you to your practice, but I will also promptly recommend to King Fonz that you each be given a special official commission and that you each have your present stipend doubled!" He walked away mumbling, "Absolutely amazing! With this it could work! It really could! It could actually work!"

He knew who was behind this and what it was about. That was clear enough – or did he? Was Mako being convinced that the ideas of someone else would work now?"

Now! Where the hell were the golems? They'd sailed away as Mako came up.

I sent them to the hill fort to send me the exact layout of the place and what's really happening out there. They can't get inside without being noticed so I'm getting an overview. I'll send some small floaters late tonight to put spy sensors around. There aren't any sorcerers out there to detect them. I'm spending a lot of the time renovating myself and adding a few new ideas so I can't take a lot of unnecessary distraction.

Z was laying on his bed to rest a bit before going down to the evemeal and to catch up on what was happening elsewhere.

"I think it's shown that Mako knows all about whatever it is," Z noted. "He mumbled something about it working – with my unit.

"So how're the guys? Anything new and different?"

*Yes. The empire's doing exceptionally well. TAR One is very good at taking over if I'm not right there and I've programmed in a lot of the things I'd do. Thing has been kidnapped – or something such – on Hades (Book 35: *Odd Couple Out*), but Kurk's not worried in any way so I won't. They seem to be having fun. Tab and Kit have a problem a lot like ours. They can't seem to locate the leader of some odd kind of interference (Book 34: *Surprise Me*). Professor Bartelt asked what we're doing and I told him we're working on the problem, but it doesn't seem to be too serious. Zianteus stopped by for a few minutes and I caught him up to date.*

"I have yet to be able to look for plants here," Z said. "If it weren't for that this would be a normal vacation on a normal world."

We're all having a nice easy time. That's a rare thing in itself where this bunch are concerned. We're usually in some kind of dire situation or other.

Maita didn't know what was really going on with Tab and Kit or on Hades so ignorance, trite as the saying is, is bliss!

Z soon went downstairs to sit with Lest at the side table to discuss whatever subjects came up. Lest was making his own tests with the moon, sun and tides and had made a chart explaining the shadow of Gaerkt on the moon and why the tides would follow a very definite schedule that could be predicted even years in advance. He also made a prediction that in only four and a half years he would be able to prove beyond any possible question that Gaerkt was round!

"Four and a half years? What? I don't quite see what you mean," Z replied, knowing full well what Lest had discovered.

"It's very simple!" Lest cried. "I have studied the tides, thus I was able to determine where Selipe was at all times in relation to Gaerkt. To do that I had to know where the sun was in relation to Gaerkt to be able to show the phase of Selipe predicted the tides perfectly. In only four and a half years Gaerkt will be in a position where it will move between the sun and Selipe for perhaps an hour or more. We can watch the shadow of Gaerkt actually move across the moon. It will be a circle and will completely hide Selipe for a few minutes when it's halfway across. It's a thing that happens periodically throughout history that was once blamed on the elementals becoming angry or as omens. The instances occur at a time and in a manner one can predict.

"Do you see?"

"I see you're trying to tell me Gaerkt is moving as well as the sun and Selipe," Z said. "I don't know if I can accept that yet.... Kant once said that, as every star and moon in all the heavens are known to be moving, only an abject fool would deny that Gaerkt is probably moving, too. He said all things in nature are patterns and Gaerkt is not the one thing in all of the world and skies that does *not* follow those patterns. He called them the 'rules of ...' of some-thing. 'Universality'?

"Do you think it will be that way?"

"I've come to much the same conclusion," Lest said. "I've studied the star we call Farst and the evening star. I even tried to make a model to explain the erratic way they seem to move. I think you know they're not in the same place at different times of the year and they seem to follow a pattern not like any other stars, yet it *is* a pattern that is repeated over a long period of time.

"I can't quite make it work. Everything moves around Gaerkt in a set pattern except them. *They* break the pattern so it's not really impossible that Gaerkt does, too."

"But if Gaerkt is moving maybe they're moving, too," Z mused. "Selipe and the sun revolve around Gaerkt, but Gaerkt's moving so it's also moving around something. That's the pattern that is *not* broken! Maybe Farst and the evening star are revolving around the same thing Gaerkt's revolving around so the pattern holds true in all things, as Kant deduced."

"I worked on that assumption," Lest replied. "I'm not sure I can credit what seems to be the truth. It will take a lot of study, but it could well be true if Gaerkt is moving. The very most basic ideas will have to change if it proves to be as it seems."

"If what's as it seems?" Z asked.

"I have predicted where the evening star will be in thirty six days," Lest said. "I used thirty six because everything must be a sphere if all the sun and stars and moon are spheres and Gaerkt is a sphere. The shadows will prove it. All are spheres. Everything in nature is, then, based on the perfect geometric shape, the one that is most efficient, the sphere. If that is true the circle is what a sphere is made of. Lots of circles. If you take a circle such as this ring and revolve it completely around it has made a sphere. If all things in nature are spheres, therefore may be described as composed of circles, Gaerkt, the sun and Selipe move in circles. That explains the regularity of the tides. Selipe moves around Gaerkt in a circle as does the sun. Gaerkt is moving in a circle. Farst and the evening star are moving in circles. If the evening star is exactly where I predict in thirty six days I know where its circle is. If Farst is where I predict in seventy two days I know where its circle is. If they are where I predict I know where Gaerkt's circle is.

"Selipe revolves around Gaerkt, but Gaerkt revolves around something else. It will surprise you what Gaerkt, Farst *and* the evening Redstar revolve around if my predictions hold!"

"And the sun?" Z asked. "Does it in its turn revolve around the same thing? Does everything, all the stars included, revolve around one thing?

"You can see what doesn't make much sense to me, but Kant claimed every circle has a center – but he was talking about wheels. He taught there has to be a spot in the center of the wheel that doesn't move when compared to the rest of the wheel, but it still moves along its own path.

"I think I've lost myself. It's too complicated for me."

Lest grinned and ordered them both a beer.

Z was right! He was a genius!

The next fifteen days went fairly smoothly, but Z knew he was being watched constantly. The golems alternated among the various people and groups, but spent most of their time with Z or Lest. The mounted guard unit he was working with became more adept at a number of things. King Fonz came with Mako to watch them in the practice several times so Z met him. King Fonz seemed puzzled about the purpose of any of it, but deferred to Mako and the head of the whole guard, General Nake, a very large (Obese), tall, coarse-featured man with an arrogant manner. The golems both took an instant dislike to him, which put Z in a bad spot, both because he found himself actually believing that the golems could really like or dislike anyone and because their remarks were more extremely acidic concerning Nake. Z wondered if Maita was controlling that, but learned later it was not. The comp running them had decided to act in that manner on its own.

The golems saved him a lot of grief when he ordered them to show Nake some respect and they made a loud show about nobody telling them what to do and only a sorcerer of the power of Kant or better dared to try! It all died down, but the time was fast approaching when he would want to irritate Nake and Mako separately to see which one ordered him sent to the hill fort. It wasn't clear whether Mako actually took any orders from Nake or vice versa. There could well be another boss over them who gave them their instructions. Z didn't feel Nake had nearly the intelligence to start such a project on his own.

He stayed away from Luxe as much as he could and she seemed to lose interest in him, thus avoiding a premature confrontation with Mako. It was getting time to start putting the big bosses into an untenable position with the people and the troops. He wished he could have di-scovered who those bosses were.

He was at a table at the inn with Viz and Wil. Lest came to join them and Z suggested he'd like to set up a sort of fair to show the people how real kirtsmen handled the animals. Lest seemed to think that was a good idea and that the people in Castiel would enjoy the educational entertainment.

"I think we should hold it as a competition," Viz said. "We talked about that once, remember? We could compete with all the other units for a prize or something and we could invite anyone else who wanted to compete to enter. The first fair would only be us, but we could have one each quarteryear or something."

"Why would you want them so often?" Lest asked.

"So we could have wagers!" Wil said. "That way the top winners in the competition could get a money prize, meaning a lot of people would want to compete."

"I think that would be a very good idea, really," Lest said, thinking. "There's ample money avaiable among the population. I don't approve of wagering when people aren't able to easily afford it, but the snows will come within twenty days and we'll then have a full quarteryear before the aftersnow season arrives for people to practice the skills you demonstrate. This will be a chance to dress up one more time before the snow season."

–Right!– No said with deep sarcasm. –Air Dome finally found an idea that could make him enough money to live on. The fact that a warrior unit shouldn't be doing that kind of thing won't figure into it at all.

–Right!–

+Now, No! We all know the warrior idea is silly and useless. It will be a wonderful chance for the people to get out into the fresh clean air for an afternoon to mingle with one another in pleasant social interaction and perhaps to find some amusement and entertainment in the sport and skills displayed. These fine relaxing times spent in close camaraderie will make the dreariness of the coming time of greys and cold a little less of a burden for....+

–Ahhhhhh, shut the gork up, Mandible Mouth! You don't even understand what you're saying yourself more than half of the time! Social interaction? Sheesh!–

"We'll design the course and decide which skills will fit best," Z continued, ignoring the golems. "The riding in units and the jumping kirts, the bowmanship, the speed runs and the multiple targets. There can be as many as six or eight different competitions and we can have levels of skill to determine the contestants in a given event."

They got a writing board and charcoal from Gild and worked on the idea for three and a half hours. Will said he'd get the crier to announce the competition on the coming rest day, which gave them six whole days to get ready. They would set up the course the following day so they could practice their special talents. Lest would figure the best way to handle the wagering with the help of Tor, who seemed to have a head for numbers. The golems would be the referees and they'd ask Mako to be the judge.

Then Z went up to bed. That should poke the firebee nest!

He wouldn't ask Mako to judge until everything was arranged. It would be very interesting to see how he reacted when he discovered he couldn't politically stop the competition. He was going to have to make a choice that he wasn't going to like no matter what.

"We'll place the targets in staggered formation," Z said. "The units will ride from the wall outward toward the road and back where the single rider competition will be to that side and will be unevenly spaced and staggered targets. The jumping shots can be set up over there and we can have a speed race along the whole outside perimeter of the field."

"My lady friend, Mam, wants me to ask you if she can put up a sweetcake bazaar," Tor said. "A lot of the women want to make pies and snacks to sell. We could charge them a centime a cake to have a bazaar stall."

"Good idea!" Z agreed. "You can put the stalls over to that side and the speed race can start and end behind them. We can put a stand right there with a marker. King Fonz is reported to enjoy the races so we'll let him have a covered seat right on the finish line. He can have the queen and Mako and anyone else he wants to invite to sit with him. The shooting courses will be over there so the arrows will have someplace to go if anyone misses a target. We *don't* want any chance of accidents! *That* would put a quick end to it!

"We can let the people who regularly like to race enter that now because the skills are already known, but we will have to limit the numbers. Maybe we can have more than one race, then have a separate race with only the winners of the first ones."

"We can have three races!" Yan suggested. "I worked with the race kirts before I was in the guard so I can arrange it. We can have one race with only the guard, one with the people who've raced at the regular fairs and one race for new entries. The last race will be against the three other winners."

"Yeah!That will let us have four wagering sessions," Tor agreed. "Very good! I cast ballot for that! We can call it the Quarterannual Kirtmanship Festival and have all competitions centered around the kirts."

"Sounds fine with me," Z replied. "We can do that. Lest says it should start snowing two days after rest day next so the timing is nearly perfect. People tell me he reads the signs very well."

"Yuh. He's as good as we've ever had around here," Yan agreed.

Maita had traced the area's prevailing weather patterns and had come to the same conclusion. Rest day would be a very pleasant, crisp, bright, dry day.

It was just four days from the first Quarterannual Kirtmanship Festival and people were already talking a lot about it so the attendance was going to be good. These kinds of things were never planned very long before they took place in this culture so the short notice wasn't unusual enough to cause comment. Nine outside contenders entered the races with five or six more expected.

Z left the units practicing a sort of jousting at hanging weighted bags he'd introduced and went to find Mako to ask him to judge the fair. The official greeter at the palace said Mako was in his offices behind the courtroom so Z waited while she went to tell him he was there and wanted a word. Lest came in at that moment from the museum chambers with the golems floating above him.

"I think perhaps you came here to invite Mako to be master judge of the festival?" Lest greeted. "I was surprised when I learned you had failed to mention it to him earlier. It would seem a natural thing to do."

"I'm proud of my unit and wanted to surprise him with the show," Z replied. "He seems to be very much part of the reason we're training the units so he can take personal pride in what they've accomplished."

–Hah, right! I'll bet the only reason Muck Mouth didn't ask him earlier is because he forgot! He'd forget his ears if it wasn't for the fact he'd notice that the wind wasn't blowing him along, as usual!–

+Now, No ... I'll bet you're right! He forgot! He does tend

to forget things if they're important enough.+

"Save your stupid bets for the festival," Z said. "Would you like to go with me to ask him to judge?"

–I wouldn't miss it for anything! We can see how Antler Ears handles the simple fact he forgot to give Judge Mako notice about the festival. Mako's gonna throw a triple conniption fit sure as the sunrise on the morrow.–

"I would like to go along," Lest requested. "I wish to speak with you later about some of the things I've discovered in my recent studies of the relative motions of the stars. We were in the book museum looking at some of the records. Some paint artists have painted the night skies and have even supplied dates so we can learn much."

The receptionist came to escort them into Mako's offices where Nake was sitting in a comfortable chair to one side.

"You wished to speak with me?" Mako asked. "If this is on a private matter Nake can wait here and we'll speak in the other office."

–Nah, it ain't private. Adipose Nose can wallow his raft aft around in the chair while we tell you of the great wonders of the day.–

+Now, No! As accurate as your descriptions may be there is certainly a more refined way to say those things. For instance you might mention that his derriere seems even broader than usual rather than call him raft aft.

+I only assume it is broader based on the fact it has become broader with each incidence when we met since our arrival in this pleasant town. If you will but....+

–Ahhh, stick it, Ammonia Breath! I'll say what I want! I don't need a lecture about the proper way to mention Blubber Bottom's bottom seems to have accumulated more blubber!–

"We wanted to request your participation in an event we've staged for rest day," Z said ignoring the golems. "I wanted it to be a surprise for you, but I assume you've already heard of our kirt festival."

"I was wondering what it was about," Mako answered. "I understand there will be kirt races and bowmanship contests. I would wonder why the guard, even a unit so exceptional as that you're training, would want to hold a festival."

"Why, to demonstrate what we've learned!" Z replied, brightly. "We'll hold competitions in all manner of skills and invite the public to compete! It'll demonstrate to everyone just how far we've advanced the arts!

"The unit wants me to ask that you do us the great honor of being the head judge for the competitions. We have some special seats for the judges and King Fonz and his guests. Everybody can wager on the competitions. It's well-known how King Fonz appreciates the kirt races and how much Nake and you like the wagerings so it'll serve a lot more of a purpose than merely the show."

+Yes! You can even have a little advantage over others because you've watched the guards practice and the guard will thence be able to demonstrate how very much a bit of direct competition can stimulate excellence!

+I recall the time in that town in Dinkard, Round Something, when they held that speed competition with the boats – you remember, No. That narrow pointy one was by far the best....+

–Ahhhhhh, yell it out your ear, Knife Nose! The wagers will make a little money for the guard and the people'll finally get some entertainment from their taxes if they *don't* get anything else.–

"You can't have the guard out there showing everyone how their training works!" Nake cried, shocked. "Not ever! There will be no kirt or weapons competition! I forbid it!"

"Oh? That would certainly be most unwise," Lest said

smoothly. "Everyone is prepared to enjoy it. If you cancel any of it now you will find yourself having to explain that to them – and we both know you can't.

"I always wondered why you were so adamant about training the guard to many things. I must wonder more now than ever. Why would anyone wish to refuse showing the skills? How will you give the units incentive to excel? What is to be lost if others know of the arts?

"I might suggest the citizens of Dinkard already know those self-same skills. That is why Zho was able to so quickly teach our guard here in Castiel. You might take note of that fact to your gain.

"You make me wonder, Nake. You make me wonder mightily about your motives. You make me wonder also at your intelligence, which is certainly not a new wonder to me.

"I think it would be most unwise for you to take this away from those men. I think they would grow to resent and despise you more than they do now. I see them soon failing to learn the arts if you deny them the pride of demonstrating them. I have oft said you are a fool, Nake. I repeat that now with emphasis."

"I will be most honored to judge the events," Mako replied with a sharp stern look at Nake. "I believe Nake fails to take into consideration how much the demon-stration of these amazing arts will stop any aggressor from ever even thinking seriously of opposing Castiel!

"I will ask that you explain each event to me very thoroughly so that I may be more fair in my judgements."

Nake sat in angry silence until Z and Lest left, the golems remaining in the room for No to soon declare, –We'll go now so Toxin Tongue can make a fool out of himself in private with only you as an audience.–

+Now, No! Nake can't help it if he has ashes for brains!

We wish you good fortunes, Mako. We'll see you when we discuss the festival. You will be delighted with the plans I am sure.

+Did you remember to invite King Fonz, Zho? We must be sure his seats are *exactly* placed for the kirt races! He has so very little chance at diversion in his station and this will be to the good of all!

+Why don't you see him while we're here? We can then go to the fields where this delightful festival will take place and be sure it is in the best of condition! It is a picturesque spot, is it not? I think the weather will be just perfect, don't you? This time of the year is so truly *delightful*! The sun is so bright and the air is crisp and cool and the refreshing zephyrs....+

−AHHHH, SHUT UP, Arsenic Breath!−

That was an oversight Yes was reminding him to repair so Z decided to detour back to tell King Fonz about the festival. Fonz invited them into his chambers to serve a mild wine and discuss the events. He seemed very pleased and noted the people needed a diversion as there weren't really any fairs or other holidays at that time of the year except the harvest festival and people were often too tired when that one took place because they had been spending all their time taking in the harvest.

City people didn't care about the festival, which had taken place a mere seventeen days ago in the country. The next festival could be combined with the Spring Festival and two could be held in the summer.

"I've been against this overtraining of the guard and the fact that we have far too many of them," King Fonz said. "Perhaps we can develop them into an emergency force with most of the training in kirtmanship and away from what appears to me to be an attack force, not one for defense. They will have use in times of natural disaster as well, being trained to cope with emergencies along with the soldier part.

"I have suggested that to Mako and Nake, but they have turned a blind eye to the idea. I do not like the way the guard seems to be becoming an attack force. It worries me greatly."

–Of course it's an attack force, Pucker Puss! Nobody could pretend it's anything else and you know it! I don't see why you don't take it on yourself to disband the whole guard.–

King Fonz grinned slightly and answered in a very serious tone, "I understand your confusion, Sludge Face. The fact is I have very little control of politics anymore. I'm basically a figurehead. The city is administered by the courts more than by the king. It is a trend for the past ten years or so."

Lest grinned at King Fonz when he innocently called No 'Sludge Face' and Z was surprised the golem didn't reply in kind. Lest later explained that the golem, No, and Fonz had traded insults from the first day. Fonz was expert at appearing deadpan while delivering his retorts. He was known to do that in court.

When Lest and Z left King Fonz the golems said they were staying with Fonz so they could enjoy some partially intelligent conversation for a change. Z knew Maita expected Nake or Mako or both to contact Fonz to try to find a way to stop or lessen the festival. The golems would be in a position to harass them enough to prevent anything from being decided.

"Well! It looks like there is to be unexpected opposition to your little festival!" Lest said when they were seated in the inn. "Nake seems very much against it."

"It's not at all unexpected," Z replied, smirking. "I've slowly learned some things about the guard and about those in top control of it so I planned this thing to be so advanced by the time they knew about it they couldn't stop it. I don't even pretend to understand what's going on here, but there's something I can only call sinister about it. It makes me wonder who has made a dangerous plan and what that plan could be.

"Do *you* know anything?"

"I share your uneasiness about it," Lest said. "I don't know what it's all about any more than you and I, too, wonder. The golems seem to think someone plans to start trying to take over other cities in an attempt to form a larger government body or something on that order. I don't understand what that would accomplish."

"I can understand it in one way," Z said. "I've seen enough of the kind of people who want to hold power over others. The more people or the larger the area the more powerful they feel or something. I don't think it could work, but a lot of people could get hurt by any such stupidity."

"The guard, no matter the training, would simply refuse, so it isn't a realistic problem in that sense," Lest pointed out.

"I wonder," Z replied slowly. "I've thought a lot about it and a lot about the differences in the way people think here and in Dinkard. I think you're right about the guard not following any such orders now, but what about if the ideas of the people are slowly changed over a period of years and there's some special growing respect for the members of the guard?"

"You mean if the guard becomes what you're making them?" Lest asked with a grin.

"You haven't looked very closely at what I'm teaching them," Z returned with his own grin. "I've taught them skills that are very good for competition and games, but they wouldn't serve any real purpose in an attack."

"When your guard can ride in in units and shoot with great accuracy anyone in their way? That would serve no real purpose in an attack?" Lest asked.

"They shoot at targets with big blue circles in the middle,"

Z pointed out. "Those targets don't move and those targets don't in any way resemble living people. They don't bleed and they don't feel pain. They don't have lifemates and families and they don't joke with you of an evening in the pub. If I wanted to train them to shoot at people from kirt back I'd make those targets in the shape of people with the target circle on the chest.

"Do you really think it would be possible to ask any of my guard to shoot at a living person and have them do it?"

"I will be stoned!" Lest cried. "You're right! They're being trained very carefully not to even take a slight chance of *accidentally* hitting anyone! You are a very intelligent man, Zho de Dinkard. You have infiltrated the enemy's war camp and made him into a friendly competitor in festival games. The training really *doesn't* lend itself to combat! I didn't see that!

"You'd better be very careful that those behind the guard who want it to be an attack force don't think of that."

"That should be less than no problem at all," Z agreed. "The skills I've taught them are very impressive to watch, particularly to anyone who knows much about kirtman-ship. The fact their talents of riding and shooting at the same time are being very highly developed is obvious. That such skills actually are large part of an effective fighting force is undeniable.

"That the men won't or can't perform against a living target won't be known until they're called upon to do so. It will then be too late to correct the oversight.

"It's my personal feeling that anything any of us can do to thwart whoever's behind this has to be done. Even the people in Dinkard aren't warlike. They just are more prone to fight anyone who they feel is invading their domain. They tend to more violence, but life isn't so easy there as it is here, so that's probably natural."

"I see again something I've seen several times before," Lest said. "It's in your speech. You speak with the high tongue like an educated man, yet you are supposed to be a barbarian from Dinkard. Your words are certainly *not* those of a barbarian! You think more than the average person and you reach some startling conclusions with little evidence to back those choices.

"You speak of training people to think in a certain pattern, yet that is something no barbarian would ever consider.

"There is an old story about King Fonz once having a younger brother who would have his throne. That brother was supposedly killed in an accident many years ago. I wonder if just perhaps your real name and identity is that of Lem de Castiel?"

"No," Z replied. "I hadn't even heard that story. I assure you I'm not from this part of Gaerkt and that I'd never been within five hundred kilometers of Castiel before I came here to seek employment in the guard. I will admit I knew something of what the guard was being trained for before I came to Castiel. I will admit I see that training as a very disturbing thing.

"Those golems represent a very great, very powerful being. That person's worried about what could happen if the people of Castiel begin to change the way they think and begin to want power. We both are greatly concerned that such a negative thing could forever change the future of this entire world and we worry as greatly that the change would become a permanent one. It might even change the Gaerkts themselves from a peaceful happy people into a people who are constantly fighting for one reason or another.

"I think you know perfectly well that thegolems could not – and *do* not – act without constant close attention. I think you can conceptualize the vast power required to activate and control them.

"Whether I'm from Dinkard or from somewhere else isn't of real importance. What I'm charged with doing *is*!"

Lest stared at him a moment, then nodded.

"Does this person know what I'm just beginning to learn of Gaerkt, Selipe and the sun?" he asked. "Does he understand the circles of the evening star and Gaerkt have the same center? Did you deliberately steer me toward studying them so I would find that truth?"

"He says the sun is the centerpoint of the circle Gaerkt and several other stars follow and that Gaerkt is the centerpoint of Selipe's circle," Z said. "He said the sun seems to be moving around a much bigger circle. He found that to be true from the very oldest art that shows the stars in positions slightly different than they are today. He studies those things and wonders greatly. He says the new questions he finds are more important than the answers and that an answer is successful only if it asks ten questions for the one answered.

"I like to think about those things, but it's far beyond my native ability to solve much of it. Once a thing's brought to my attention I can often carry it on, but I am *not* a great problem solver! The problem has to be something that is within my, I guess you could call it, personal interest.

"I don't think the golems were trying to steer you anywhere. You had thought of much of that before we ever met and I know I didn't try to direct your studies in any way. My job here has only the one object. To stop this insane desire for trouble among a few people before it destroys Castiel if not all of Gaerkt!"

"If someone has thought of changing how people think and has been successful in doing it I don't believe you *can* stop them," Lest said. "We can hope it isn't anything like that and that our worst fears about such things are unfounded.

"I know of one thing they cannot stop. The festival will be

held!"

"The riders will come along the center of the targets and will fire at as many of them as they can," Z said to Mako when the festival was to begin in less than an hour. "Your judging should be based on how accurately they find the center mark on the targets and how many they find as well as the speed and kirtmanship they show in the run. There are two units of four kirtsmen each, to follow. That will be harder to judge because you will have to consider how well they work and move together as a team, not only the speed, accuracy and smoothness of the individual.

"The lance striking is much simpler and is mostly to be an entertainment because the rider is as apt to knock himself from the kirt as he is to be able to hit the hanging target.

"The thing to consider there is that the rider must strike the target with just enough force to dislodge it from a kirt if it's a man on kirt back without striking it so directly the long lance penetrates. If a lance is stuck in the first enemy it's useless from that point onward.

"King Fonz will judge the kirt races. He enjoys that. You have the other little exhibitions such as the jumping and shooting and the water tags."

"Water tags?" Mako asked. "I don't know that one."

"We have the watering pond in the center of the grounds," Z said. "We have the units go into the pond riding on kirt back and try to dislodge one another. The last man on kirt back in each unit will meet the winner of the other unit to see who's last to remain mounted. They can work together at first, but only one will be the winner in the tags so it might not be smart to do so. It tests the reflexes of the individual rider as well as his ability to improve his chances in any contest. It requires that he thinks.

"The wagering will be posted before each meet and will

stop before the competition begins. The more people who place bets the higher the prize to the participant so they'll make a good show of it because that'll mean higher prizes in the next meet. It'll also make every one of them more determined to become *better* at any skill than the others so works in several ways at once.

"The object of this fair is far more than merely a festival. It gives the guards a strong incentive to improve. I don't think there's a better way to make men become good at a thing than personal reward.

"The main other objective is to get the people in the area of the city to learn to admire the skills we're teaching. You must admit that you tend to admire those men for the things you've seen while they're only practicing!"

"Very true," Mako agreed. "It should prove a positive thing in several ways. Nake is worried about this because he thinks it shows the people the things they're learning so it will also show others how to arrange defenses against it."

"Oh? I always thought defense was the primary objective in the training," Z replied innocently. "It doesn't matter. I don't see how knowing about those arts would make them easier to defense. The skill takes a great deal of work and training so they can't expect to do anything against it."

"If they know the units will charge in a certain pattern they'll situate their own troops to be able to accurately shoot them before they can do anything," Mako said. "I can see that point."

"But you don't know what I've planned to train them to do so the opposition won't be able to do that!" Z said triumphantly. "This training isn't all there is to it – by far! If we're to be effective we have to keep anyone else from knowing some parts of the plan. The part this will demonstrate will lead others into making mistakes that will ensure their failure against the troops. Perhaps I *want* people to think this is all. Perhaps I *want* defense for this particular kind of charge under these conditions planned and in place if anyone ever attacks us. Perhaps that's part of the whole plan."

Mako looked at him strangely a moment then, grinned a small grin and mumbled, "I wonder exactly who you're doing what to! I wonder what your real motives are in this! I wonder much about too many things where you're concerned, Zho of Dinkard! I wonder mightily!

"Just what *are* you teaching these men?"

"I'm teaching them how to seize and hold power," Z answered.

"Ah, yes! True! But for whom?" Mako asked, watching Z closely.

"It is a puzzle, isn't it?" Z asked. "Maybe it's for one or maybe it's for another. Maybe it's for several or maybe it's for many."

"Ah! And maybe also you're playing a very dangerous game," Mako warned. "Maybe I do respect you for that. It's always possible someone else has the rules in mind as firmly as do you. That someone could well know a few things you don't.

"Consider sources of information. Think long and hard before you do anything that could bring you grief, my friend. I admit to having a great respect and even a liking for you, but you can't hope to hold control of all of it even with your friends, the golems."

"I don't want to control anything," Z replied. "I want this done so I can move on to other things in other places. I wasn't saying I wanted power, Mako. I don't. This is a study for me and I'll be gone. It wasn't even my own idea to come here. I could never bring myself to stay in one place for even as much as one year – though I may not be able to leave here for that long or a little longer.

"Life isn't always the way we want it to be. Some things we do because we must."

"I would ask about the sorcerer who made those golems, but know it would be to no resolve," Mako replied. "You say he is dead, but that can't be. His power would also be dead.

"I think I fear that sorcerer mightily. I think I fear his use of power."

"I will tell you the sorcerer who built those golems isn't the power who directs them now," Z replied.

"Then I know a much greater fear," Mako said soberly. "It means there is a power greater than that which made them."

"Maybe," Z agreed. "Maybe it's only a trick, anyhow."

"Then I fear the power of the trickster to make us all think in ways that will do his bidding," Mako said. "It nears time to start the festival."

The golems chose that time to come overhead and for No to say cheerily, −Time to start the show, Fang Face! You and Noodle Nose will be so kind as to take your desig-nated seats before I feel compelled to start the festivities myself!−

+Now, No! Show a little breeding! Just tell them it's time to start! There is no need to ruin such a fine day with....+

−*What* breeding? You want I should show some breeding?! In case it escaped your myopic miniscule attention we're cast bronze golems! Where in all the nine hells does any *breeding* come into it? Sheesh!−

"You two shut up," Z ordered. "Come on, Mako! Let's get the games going! The public awaits us!"

Z slipped away behind the bazaar stands and said, "Maita?"

I caught it. It could be coincidence, but he came a little too close to saying it, didn't he?

"Now I have to know why," Z replied. "Was it something someone overheard? There were plenty of people around who could have."

It remains to be seen. We'll have to set a trap.

"Well, Viz won the singles in target riding and the elite unit won the group," Z explained to King Fonz as they watched the men wrestling and playing in the pond. (The water tag game had turned into a fun fest that reminded Z of the times he and his friends had carried each other on their shoulders in the water to play – which was good. The wagering was good on the game and everyone was having great fun.) "I was surprised at how close the group shooting charge really was. They each did more than I had thought they could!"

"I wish I could stop being king for one afternoon and go out there and join them in the pond," Fonz said. "The hardest thing about this job is not being able to join into the games people always play. It just isn't any fun!"

"You're not allowed to ever give up the throne are you?" Z asked.

"If I could give it up I'd *be* in that pond!" Fonz replied, with feeling. "I want to thank you for an afternoon that has been delightful. It's good to be out here away from that castle. It won't be long before the snows come and we'll all have to spend entirely too much time indoors.

"Ah-ha! I won that one! Now if Jon can only win the triple match!

"I hope you'll forgive my decreeing the people could join the water tag if they wanted. I think it's best that as many as possible participate in most of it. I knew Jon was big enough and quick enough to win this with the people, but he might not have such a chance against the two from your unit. I bet on him anyhow."

"The units have an advantage because their kirts have been trained so well to follow their commands," Z agreed. "I think it was a very good idea to invite a public team. I wanted to invite the people into a lot more of it, but Nake seemed opposed to all of it. He seems opposed to ... too many things."

"Nake is someone I'll warn you you must never trust, considering that we can't so easily be overheard here," Fonz said. "He is a man without humor and is physically ugly, which is a very poor combination. It is sad I could not choose my own head of the guard. It would *not* be one such as he!"

He stood and called for Jon to come take his prize, a ring Fonz had made for the winner of each event. A winner would keep the ring until he was beat at the games or until he won six times, in which case it was his. He would also get one fourth of the profits from the wagering booth for that event.

The jousting was held next to allow the water tag win-ners to rest, then the tags were held among the three. Yan won that event without too much trouble. Z stayed with Fonz until all the races were run. Wil won the first race, Jorg, a citizen, won the second race, Kyl, another citizen, the third and Vik the fourth.

Fonz stood after the fourth race to announce that the four winners would now race a final and that the trainer, Zho de Dinkard, would also compete at the king's request.

Z hadn't planned to participate in any event, but he had no special skills as a kirt racer so couldn't very well refuse. He got his mount, brought it around and waited.

The five riders started together, then Z held back a bit until they were approaching the finish. He and Kyl crossed so closely that King Fonz said he couldn't call the race fairly as he had bet on Zho. No one else could determine with any certainty who won the race so Fonz said there would have to be another race between the two – with the golems as judges! There could be no claim of bias if he won a close bet!

The people loved the idea so they asked the golems, who had been constantly harassing Nake mercilessly at the time, to do the honors.

+Why, we're greatly honored that you would think of us! I promise to be fair and impartial and to do my utmost to ensure that a true and proper result is promulg....+

–AH, SHUT UP, GONGHEAD! We'll judge the crummy race! I can guarantee you I'LL be honest!

–Farthead loses! Give Kyl the prize!–

"They haven't run the race yet, Toad Lips," Fonz said. "I think we can depend on the two of you to be honest. Despite what people may think you have never lied that I have discovered. You're obnoxious, but honest."

–You, I like, Liver Lips.

–On your line! Get the kirts to the line! We ain't sitting in this heat all day! If you're gonna race, then race!–

Z and Kyl lined up and waited until Yes yelled, +Start!+

He couldn't hold back now because Kyl would know the basic strategy and would pace him too far, thus tiring his mount so he stayed about even for awhile, then raced for a short sprint at the halfway marker, drawing ahead. Kyl speeded up and he dropped back until they were even again.

The mounts weren't fresh, having just run the first race so Z waited until they were near the finish line to make his move. The guard kirt was trained in endurance. The work kirt wasn't, so Z won by about half a length. He received the ring and went back to the stables with his kirt. Kyl came to congratulate him and he explained how to better train the fine mount Kyl rode for more endurance in the next game if there was a tie. Fonz walked up while they were talking and said he'd have the golems judge the events if they were around because they said they could detect the winner with special powers. "They told me they can slow-see," Fonz explained. "They can make their minds work much faster than normal people so can see even the finest hair's width of difference. I know they don't lie, despite their other faults."

"They can't lie," Z agreed. "It was something Kant made into them. It's their *worst* fault!"

"That's probably too true," Kyl said. "They say the craziest things about old Nake, but you have to admit it's all true."

They chatted for a few minutes, then Z went back to the inn – where a guardsman handed him a note from Nake. He'd been given orders to report to the hill fort to train the next units in secrecy.

There were several places that one could have come from so he'd been thwarted – for the moment – in his plan to use that to see who was running this show!

"This is Captain Kad, who'll be in *full* charge of the whole operation," Nake said, introducing Z to the people he would be working with at the hill fort. "You will answer to him in all things.

"You'd better understand that we must maintain order here. There are dangerous criminals being held here to keep them away from Castiel and its citizens as well as regular castle guard personnel.

"In short, Captain Kad is your superior officer and you will follow his orders exactly."

–I think you're the real definition of musclehead all by yourself. You damned well don't have any brains in there! Did it ever occur to your royal Fatass that Zho isn't a member of the guard and that you can't give orders like that? Remember that Mako hired him to *teach* the guards, Fishpuss!–

+I am forced to agree with you, as disagreeable as that fact is. The term 'musclehead' fits him exceptionally well if one understands that lack of use of a muscle leads to rapid atrophy. I think I'll just call him Flabhead!+

"You two knock it off!" Z demanded. "He can't help it.

"No does have a point, but I'll wait to see how this works out before I take any action against your misplaced arrogance."

"You have the choice of taking your orders from Captain Kad as a member of the guard or as another prisoner among the criminals!" Nate said sharply. "I can have you detained for breach of security! That festival was stupid!"

–Maybe you should give Lard Brains a quick and very pointed lesson in hand-to-hand combat. It would be kinda interesting to see just how long he could hold out against someone less than half his size and in ten times as good a condition!–

+Again, I defer to your conclusions! Amazing!

+It might also be interesting to see how long it takes all that lard to heal! Maybe we could melt it down and run it all together again into another amorphous lump like it is now and no one would notice the rearrangement!+

"I've never seen you two agree on two things on the same day and that's three," Z said. "Is this some special occasion I should know about?"

–We both find Frog Breath obnoxious. Our disgust throws our timing off–

"I'll take orders from Captain Kad so long as it suits me," Z replied conversationally to Nake, who was now truly livid – with no recourse against the golems. He dared not challenge them as he once tried. The result of that was a joke among most everyone in Castiel. "When I decide to leave I'll leave. If you can stop me you don't need my teaching. It should be a fair test, don't you think?

"Show me my quarters and introduce me to my unit."

Nake was more angered than ever, but knew it would be worse than foolish to give Z reason to act on the golems' suggestion to demonstrate a little of the things he was to teach the guard. He looked at Kad, who stood looking back to him.

"Now!" Z snapped. "I don't care to stand here all day!"

Nake turned to lead them away and Z noticed the quick grin crossing Kad's face. Apparently Captain Kad didn't think much of Nake either, but no one he'd met to this point had any respect for him.

"There will be only the four men on this team," Nake declared as they moved along the hallway. "You will teach them to instruct other units. Perhaps you won't be able to advertise what they know so easily that way."

"One more little remark like that and I'll be on my way," Z said. "You make it obvious how very little truth you're telling anyone. If the purpose of the guard being trained in this way was actually for defense you'd be more than happy for everyone in the whole damned world to know they didn't have a wet perkfeather's chance to stand against them! Not for a moment!"

"You don't appear to tell the whole truth to any great extent yourself!" Nake replied. "I wonder what you're teaching the men and why! Is it that you want them to be a strong fighting force or is it that you want them to be incapable of acting as a guard in any manner?"

"Maybe I want them to be a strong fighting force – but not against the ones who you plan," Z suggested. "Maybe not. Quite a puzzle, isn't it?"

"I don't even pretend to understand any of it," Kad complained. "The arts you've already taught those guards-men in Castiel seem unquestionably to be of great advantage to a fighting force. I saw the kirt festival and was truly amazed at how effective they could be. As you stated, *no* one could hope to stand against such a trained force.

"I'm afraid I must share Nake's confusion as to why you then place them in competition where everyone can see what they know. If the enemy knows about it they might easily defense against it."

–Hey, Rock Head! Maybe you can't see the one thing that's so damned obvious to Fart Face and us! Maybe there's one tiny little detail here that nobody wants to see.

–Concentrate! Clear your mind!

–*What* enemy?–

+And the purported purpose of this whole thing was for the guard to be defensive so why would you worry about others being able to defend against *them*? Tell me what sense that makes in regard to the former point. If they were supposed to be trained as an offensive force you should have told Zho. He could have trained them in a very different way. Those arts are not the same and the necessary strategies to be employed are radically different – but you will not have known of or considered strategy, which can be more important in a battle than any amount of training.

+If you remember that place in South Island on the long....+

–GHAAAH! Here we go again! A meandering trip through the cluttered mess that serves for your, excuse the exaggeration, mind!

–The *question* was, 'What's that guard really for?'–

There was another quick grin at Nake's back as Kad shrugged. They turned into a sort of mess hall where four men were seated at a bench table drinking hot cav. The captain called them to attention and said, "This is Zho, who will be your trainer.

"Zho, this is Sto (Clapping each on the shoulder as he was introduced, as was the custom), Eil, Jok and Tig. They are already highly accomplished kirtsmen."

Z looked them over, nodded and went to the kettle to pour himself a mug of cav. He then sat with them for a few minutes longer chatting about Dinkard. Nake was completely omitted from their conversation so he soon left and Kad showed Z to his quarters after he finished his cav.

"I can intuit you don't care for Nake anymore than I do," Z said. "He really is the north part of a southbound kirt isn't he?"

"It's part of any political system that you have to put up with such as the Nakes of the world if you want to hold your job," Kad agreed. "I find it best to say `yes' to about anything he suggests, then to do as I think best as soon as he goes away again. No need to complicate life because of some swamptoad like that. I heard about his confrontation with the golems in Castiel. Fifty people had to tell me about it. Everyone likes the golems for that little turn-around. They get a lot of respect from people who know Nake.

"Do you actually control them or are they independent of your control?"

"I wish they were under my control so I could make them stay away from me most of the time," Z answered. "They're usually good company on my wanderings and can keep me out of trouble in a lot of ways, but they keep me IN trouble when we're around towns or cities."

"I think I'll like them," Kad decided. "I think I like you. I like anyone who stands steady against Nake's type while I also think it a bit foolhardy. He *does* have a lot of power at the court – both the king's and the civil court.

"Do you know where the golems are now?"

"They'll look over the fort and probably stay around the men to chat and get to know them," Z replied. "You'll discover they like to instigate arguments. If you don't want to get involved in that act simply ignore them. If you don't answer they go away."

"King Fonz seemed to enjoy replying to their insults with his own quips," Kad agreed. "They harassed Nake every time they were near him, but didn't stay around him. He wouldn't reply to them at all."

"I wish to the hells I knew why they dislike him so violently," Z said. "It's rare for them to be nearly that adamant about anything. They're usually right about things – don't let them *ever* know I said that – and I'd like to know what it is with Nake. It worries me. It worries me greatly when they agree in any small degree about anything and most of all when it's about such as that one."

"I suppose it's mostly because he's such a poor excuse for a Gaerkt," Kad said. "And don't ever let him know I said *that*!

"I'll let you settle in and get some rest. You can set your own program with the men and do what you think best. I don't pretend to know how to train anyone the way you trained those men in Castiel. I won't interfere."

He went out to find Nake to get his further orders and to send him on his way back to Castiel while Z laid back on the surprisingly comfortable bunk. Maybe he'd found an ally here in Kad like the one he'd found in Castiel in Lest. Maybe things would work out for the best. Maybe he'd soon find what this was really about and who was really behind it.

He'd have to be very careful. He didn't know who he could trust here even moreso than in Castiel. That, after all, was the point!

"The first thing we'll do here is design a place to practice and set it up," Z decided the next morning at the dawnmeal. His four students joined him at his request and he invited Kad to sit with them.

"Will you want your practice area right by the fort?" Kad asked.

"I'll ride around the whole area," Z said. "We'll find the places most like what a force might find in a battle and set them up. Part of it will necessarily be near the fort. That's unavoidable. We won't change much of anything. Just put targets around for the most part. We might put in some jumps and water hurdles or that sort of things. The season will be a big factor. You do *not* use the same techniques in snow as on a grassy plain.

"I'll teach these men a lot of the things I taught the units in Castiel, but I'll also teach them a number of very different things for very different conditions."

"But I thought those city units knew about everything it was possible to know!" Kad cried. "I was amazed at their skills and talents!"

"They're at a city," Z replied. "It's a very different thing to have to defend a city than it is to defend a fort. It's different again to have to defend open areas or farms that aren't walled or fortified. This will be a very different thing. These men will know the things the units in Castiel know, but will also know several other arts. I taught those men in Castiel in only sixty four days. The things I'll teach this group will take about a year and a half, but they'll be the finest unit on all of Gaerkt!

"Just to infuriate such as Nake I'll probably challenge the Castiel group next festival day. The arts needed for those meets will be the same for them as for us so we'll be able to compete fairly. The other things we'll learn here won't generally apply to those games and it's probably better if we don't make up any games to use them. The arts you'll need for this kind of thing are far more dangerous, so I won't hold it against any man who wants out. I happen to like danger, but I'm from Dinkard!"

It would be in character for him to brag and strut a little so he'd make it a point to do that now and again. It would spur the men on to take their training more seriously because they could feel a certain pride in it. As back on Earth facing grave danger with a touch of disdain was considered a masculine trait and it would make the whole thing more exciting. He would also teach them a lot of things that looked good, but that had little value in actual combat, things that could be made into games of skill later.

There wasn't much chance any of it would ever be needed in actual warfare because, again, he was going to teach these men things that would be used only in good-natured competition and not in political adventurisms.

He was also certain Kad didn't know who or what was behind this anymore than he did.

Where were the golems and what were they doing? He didn't want to contact Maita until he knew a lot more about where there might be surveillance posts. It was altogether possible his quarters were being watched and listened to. Nake would see to that.

"We'll place the jumps along here where there are natural little hills," Z suggested, drawing them onto his big map. He'd carefully laid it all out on a large piece of cured skin and had made various symbols for the various things such as targets, jumps, water holes, rocks, etc. He also had several small maps of certain of the other nearby areas that would offer very different problems.

"We can put targets along the top of the wall all along this side and put up skins behind them so none of the arrows fall on the people inside if anyone misses a target. In a very short time it's going to be rare for anyone to miss.

"We're also going to have to learn some very difficult moves to fight against a fort, moves that aren't used against a city.

"Now! Let's go out toward those hills over there and on to the mountains. We don't have anything else to do yet so we'll find a good place to set up our camp to train in the mountains themselves. We can work back toward the fort, training in the hills and forest. There's a bit of a plain over to the east where we can learn a little about that kind of thing, but it's not as good as I'd like."

The golems came floating casually overhead to listen. They made no immediate smart remarks, indicating to Z that maybe they'd found something.

"There's a river over past the plains we'll use to learn the water techniques," he continued. "The most difficult place to fight, believe it or not, is on the banks of a river. Your kirt isn't so sure-footed and is prone to jerk about, but you'll learn about that in due time. This kind of area where there are so many rocks is hard on the kirts. You must *never* run into such an area. If the kirt were to trip or goes lame you're the target instead of the archer. If you flip and are thrown the rocks will kill you as fast as any arrow.

"We use a special formation to fight in such areas and we much move slowly. If you ever find yourself in a position of having to defend strictly for survival find such an area and get into it. The disadvantages are then transferred back to your adversary and you're going to be much better bowmen than most!

"Would you golems agree to that?" (Might as well go for a bit of comic relief.)

–The whole idea's stupid, Bladder Brain! You know perfectly well there won't ever be any need for this idiotic training! It looks like you could find a better way to waste time.–

+Now, No! Be nice! It's a lovely day, just cool enough to be brisk and invigorating, yet is warm enough to make one dream of perfect beauty and tranquility I sometimes wish we could ride a kirt out in such truly beautiful weather to enjoy the solitude of the countryside and the beauty of nature's bounty! The crispness in the air, the coolness of the breeze. They combine to enlighten one with a sense of true....+

–AHHH! SHUT THE NINE HELLS UP, NEWT NOSE! It's going to be snowing before dawn tomorrow! We can float around anywhere we want in case that escaped your pitiful little excuse for a mind! We don't have to wander around on some dumb smelly beast that craps every third step! *Sheesh*! You never learn!–

+Now, No! A little snow to clear the air and put its white, brisk, clean blanket of autumn across the hills is absolutely and truly delightful! I was speaking allegor-ically so there's no need to be so negative! If you'll look at the bright side of things you'll find life to be so much more pleasant!

+Observe these happy people before you riding through the cool quietness of the countryside contemplating the deeper meanings of life. A little snow won't detract from....+

–Will you *please* shut the hells up for once in your existence! Snow's water and water dulls our finish, Frog Eyes! The pleasant thing would be to be inside a warm *dry* building! Let these animal types parade around out here in snow and slush. I'll take a dry warm room over the cool wet de*light*ful meadow any day, thank you!

–You can sure be stupid sometimes! All the time. I really shouldn't be surprised how stupid anymore. You spend all your time demonstrating it, Bladdermouth!–

"You didn't answer the question," Z replied placidly while the men chuckled at the golems.

–I did! I said the whole thing's stupid, Fish Breath! You never listen! With those ears that you could use to fly if you flapped them you'd think you could hear a plain simple statement of fact!–

+I think it's well that we be prepared for any eventuality. Your plans, what we've heard of them to date, seem quite appropriate, Zho. It's far better to have a thing and not need it than it is to need a thing and not have it. That also applies to any skills garnered through diligent practice and attention to details.

+Remember the time in Kistle when you had that slub thing hanging from your pack that you kept saying was nothing more than extra weight and how glad you were to have it there when that growlerbeast came....+

–JUST SAY THE HELL YOU NEED THINGS YOU DIDN'T EXPECT ONCE IN AWHILE! The rest of it is kirt droppings! It's all a waste!–

+That's not the point! Nothing in life is wasted! One never

knows when or where a thing will be needed. It's all a matter of perspective! Always be prepared and you won't be disappointed in retrospect! Zho knows that. He, at least, is prepared for....+

–I know when some things are not needed, Jabber Jaws! One of them is positioned just behind and to my right!–

+My point exactly! I'm not *needed* right now, but isn't it nice to know I'm here for when I AM needed? Wouldn't it be better....+

–AHHHHHHHHHH!– No cried as the floater drifted off toward the fort. Yes was saying, +Now, No! I've told you and told you about being so negative! You tend to spend a mite too much of your time looking on the dark side of things! The gold is in the mine if you will *look* for it! I know there's not....+

–Shut *up*! For the untold mercy of the great elementals, SHUT UP, Turd Lips!–

+Now, No....+

–I can't stand it! I just can't *stand* it!–

The unit was enjoying the show. They were all laughing and sympathizing with one or the other of the golems, most saying No had the hardest part because they knew just how irritating the goody-goody type could be – and there was no way for either to escape the other.

What was that about?

They moved toward the mountains. Z was wondering which parts of that exchange were supposed to be a message to him. He was sure the part about never knowing when a given talent would be needed was part of it. He understood the part about riding out in solitude, but that wasn't going to be easy.

The golems would be there when they were needed, which might have something to do with the weapons built into that floater. He had the ones in his own shield.

Get inside a warm dry building. It was going to snow during the night and that was somehow important. The golems could float anywhere so perhaps they'd overheard something.

The trouble with a lot of Maita's messages was that no one could understand them. It was going to be something his talents built up through diligent practice were going to be needed for. Oh, well. When it came, it came. He'd have to be ready.

Maybe he could manage to get away from the men far enough to use the com.

The clouds were building up solidly ahead and seemed to be moving toward them too rapidly. Should they go back?

They could be into the mountains in an hour or so, take a quick look around and get back long before dark so they moved onward. They were entering the mountains near a sort of rocky low escarpment when snow suddenly began falling. The warmer air caused quite a lot of fog to be mixed with it.

"To the mountain!" Z called. "We can find shelter."

"I never saw a snowstorm come up near this fast!" Eil said. "I can't see you guys hardly at all and we're not even five meters apart!"

"This is mostly compressed limestone rock in these mountains," Z lectured. "Stay close and we'll get against the lee side of the mountain ahead. We should be able to find some kind of overhang or cave or something, then we'll build a fire."

They stayed close and moved toward the mountain.

Okay. The golems were trying to warn him to get inside, but they could have been plain about that. There was no reason the golems couldn't know about weather. They knew he couldn't get away from others at the fort, but had said that about a solitary ride and they hadn't told him about the storm coming. They promised they'd be close if they were needed, yet they hadn't warned him about the storm later – so they were being watched and this was exactly what he was supposed to do.

Why?

"There's a sort of wall over to our left where the snow's blowing over and not in," Tig suggested. "Might be enough to stay out of the weather unless it changes wind direction or something."

"Let's get as close as we can and ride along it a ways," Z suggested. "We'll find a good place and start a fire.

"Did you hear something?"

He thought he heard a yell from the right and behind them, but couldn't be sure with the noise of the wind.

"Prob'ly the wind," Jok answered. "Makes a lotta odd noises hereabouts. Sound don't carry much'n these here kinda snow mush and wet air conditions."

They moved slowly ahead until they came to a tangle of dead trees. Z went around and came back to say they could proceed on past them.

They went on for another hundred meters and came to a large opening where a huge wedge-shaped chunk had fallen out of the mountain leaving a cave about thirty meters deep and ten wide. It was high, but should afford them good protection unless the wind changed direction a full hundred eighty degrees.

"Sto and Jok. Go back to those dead trees and bring us back plenty of firewood we can keep dry," Z ordered. "Use the heavy blankets to wrap as much as the two kirts can carry. Tig, start a fire back inside in that corner with the stuff laying around. There should be plenty of tinder in those leaves that's so dry it's brittle. Use the carry tins to start melting some snow for water. Watch for stingerbugs in those places.

"Eil, we'll survey the close area. I don't think there are any dangerous animals in this area, but we don't want to get a surprise before morning if anything wants to share the cave."

The men moved quickly to attend their assigned duties. Z wanted to be alone, but safety had to take precedence over whatever Maita knew. He'd either get help or a report if it became of overriding importance.

Within half an hour they had plenty of wood laid by and a nice little blaze going. It was reasonably comfortable in the little cave with the hard wind blowing steadily away. Jok knew the mountains well and soon came in carrying two large rabbit-like animals and some large potato-like tubers. He expertly skinned the animals and dropped them into the carry tin, poured on some water, then peeled the tubers and dropped them in.

"Be done whenst they done boiled mebbe an hour," Jok announced. "You kin tell 'cause the groundbread tubers'll get crispy soft. Take 'em out afore they's too soft. They gets mushy. I got salt. Allus carry salt no matter where you's goin' er you'll be eatin' bland food when you cud be eatin' good."

They lounged around the cave while their food was cooking talking about their homes and the kinds of storms that used to come up – but few so suddenly. The food was delicious. It was as good as that served in the restaurants in Castiel. Z mentioned it, saying food cooked out like that was always more to his taste.

"They done put all kindsa crap in ut in their cities," Jok said. "Takes the flavor out'n all you kin taste is the crap. This here's natural 'n tastes ut!"

"I've noticed that fact. Most of the natural things are different in Dinkard," he explained. After all, he should know that kind of thing!

Z could see why they called the big tubers groundbread. It tasted like the potato bread he used to eat on Earth and the tubers were shaped somewhat like bread. He slipped a piece of it into the analyzer on the floater to be sure it was safe, then punched for it to be retained. Maita could synthesize it to perfection.

Strange. He could remember the taste of potato bread that he hadn't tasted in more than three hundred years!

They laid in their blankets and had a good quiet night's sleep. The storm abated about an hour before dawn and the sun came out about an hour later as the clouds moved on away toward the fort. There was a clean blanket of snow over everything and it was bitingly cold, but there wasn't any wind to drive the cold so it wasn't uncomfort-able to any great degree.

"We might as well head back to the fort," Z said. "We aren't going to be able to practice anything out here until the spring season comes that we can't practice as well close to the fort.

They rode along for almost half an hour when Z caught sight of the floater over to their right. It was hovering out where he could see it plainly enough. The only reason the others hadn't was because they didn't look that way.

It was there to be seen. Deliberately. Something or someone was in the copse of scrubby conifers below it. Z looked around, then called for the unit to halt.

"What's the matter, Zho?" Tig asked.

"I see something nobody from Dinkard would miss," Z answered. "It's going to be part of your training to see such things so you look around and tell me."

They looked around carefully, but no one saw anything in particular so Z pointed toward the copse where the golems were now nowhere in evidence.

"Hey! They's some tracks inna snow there!" Jok cried. "Mebbe somebody done got caught inna storm'n needs help!"

"No way!" Z warned sharply. "Use your brains! That's not what's going on here!"

"Those tracks were put down there after the storm so they weathered it all right," Tig said. "They went in there *after* the snow stopped or there wouldn't be any tracks."

"What is there to hide from out here?" Z asked.

"There isn't anything at all to hide from for at least ten kilometers in any direction except the fort!" Eil answered.

"So they're hiding from us," Z pointed out. "Now you learn something about the training: First is to assume that anyone who would hide from you in such a situation means you no good. Be alert!"

He urged his kirt forward after reaching up to untie the string that fixed his bow to his shoulder and to slip the cover off the quiver. The men were immediately nervous and tended to hang back a little, but they were also excited. It was plain Z thought they were in danger – and they weren't used to that at all!

When they were about as close to the copse as their trail would naturally take them, Z suddenly leaned down flat along his kirt's back, yelling "Down!" at the same instant. The others automatically followed his lead. An arrow whistled across his back missing him by no more than ten centimeters. He rose on his kirt to the attack position, flipped his bow and arrow out and into shoot position, yelled, "Bonzai!" as he spurred the mount forward, let an arrow fly into the copse and immediately placed another. A man ran from the copse, firing another crossbow arrow in his general direction as he simultaneously fired back. His arrow went directly through the attacker's heart.

He rode up and dropped off the kirt at the side of the body.

The other four rode up to stare down at the body, Eil and Sto looked positively sick while Tig stayed back a bit. Jok rode up to look down at the body.

"Ut's Kak from the fort!" he cried. "What'n stars uz the fool doin' shootin' ut you?"

"I suppose he had orders or was paid to shoot me," Z replied. "People like Nake don't like me very much and might think the best thing would be for me to not be around here anymore.

"Should we dig a hole and bury him out here or should we take him back to the fort and let them see just what happens to people who would try to kill Zho de Dinkard?"

"You ain't sure what'n done sent Kak out here?" Jok asked.

"If I knew I'd ride in and put a few arrows in his ass!" Z replied.

"Why'nt we dig a hole in the trees an' nobody knows nothin'?" Jok said. "Ain't nobody liked 'ih nohow. Won't miss 'im!"

"You know, it might be a good idea to see who wants to know if maybe we saw Kak out here somewhere," Z said, with a grin.

They buried him in the copse, agreed that no one saw him and headed on.

The golems came floating out to greet them as they rode up asking how they liked being caught out in such lovely weather. Z said they were quite comfortable, thank you. They were always fully prepared for such minor inconveniences. They were good survival lessons any troop should know before they strayed more than ten meters from the fort.

"How are things here?" Z asked.

+Well, there were some visitors after you rode out to make your area maps. You missed the very best kinds of people! There was King Fonz, Lest, Mako and Captain Gyr! There was also Nake, but I don't see how he could possibly be considered among the better kinds ... of anything.+

–Yeah! The whole silly bunch ran around all directions keeping the whole place in an uproar! Barge Ass was trying so hard to impress Fonz I thought he'd have heart failure! Mako was trying to find out what you were up to out here, Lest was having stupid philosophical discussions with these clowns here who couldn't understand a word he said ... it was great fun! We couldn't keep up with them all!–

They didn't know who ordered his death. Great. They still knew nothing.

"We were out to map the mountain area so we would know where to practice," Z said. "You knew that. Why not tell them that and let them concentrate on other things?"

+Oh, No told them where you were heading, but they weren't at all satisfied with that. They wanted to know exactly and even suggested No and I go out to find you, but No didn't want to get wet and have to spend the time polishing and it's none of their concern so long as you're training the men anyway. I wouldn't have told them anything. It's not any of their business, really. All they have to worry about is IF you train the unit, not where or how. There are those times when people overstep....+

–Cork it, Dumbdome!–

All of that crowd knew where to expect him. Still, the whole bunch of suspects – and the head of it may not have even been with them!

"Well, we'll have to wait for the spring weather to practice in the mountains so they can watch if they want," Z replied. "I'm sort of glad we missed them."

–You didn't, Blubber Mouth. They had to stay because of the storm and won't go back to Castiel until after midmeal.–

"You men get a little rest – and don't repeat anything to anyone about anything that happened after we left the cave this morning," Z instructed. "I'll go report to Kad so he won't have to listen to a lot of noise from Nake."

They cleaned and fed the kirts, put them in their stalls, then Z went inside where he couldn't see any unusual reactions to his presence. He talked awhile with King Fonz, who was quite pleased that he had such good men in his unit, then with Lest about general things.

At midmeal no one mentioned anything at all about Kak or asked if there was any trouble on the way back to the fort. After the meal the group from Castiel got in their carriage to head back to the city as a fort guard came to say Kak hadn't reported for duty at the midshift and that he wasn't on the fort grounds anywhere. There was a kirt missing early in the morning, but it had wandered back a few minutes before midmeal.

Captain Kad was furious that Kak wasn't on duty there and demanded he be found and brought to headquarters for discipline. He'd had enough subordination from Kak and if he didn't have an acceptable explanation for not reporting for duty he might end up in a cell for a year! It was getting near time to convene a tribunal for that one!

Lest said he'd send a seeking spell if Kad liked, but Kad said Kak was probably laying out somewhere smoking dizzyweed. He'd been caught at that more than one time before. It was why he reacted so strongly when Kak was reported as absent from duty.

Lest made a powder with a piece of Kak's clothing in it and set it afire. It smoldered in a perfectly normal manner and Lest seemed somewhat confused and repeated the process. The exact same thing happened.

"The person whose clothing you gave me is dead," Lest said. "Did those things come from another who died and who left them to this Kak person?"

"No. They're issue," Kad answered.

"Then he's dead," Lest stated positively and climbed up into the king's carriage, apparently dismissing the whole thing from his mind. He started talking with Fonz about the weather conditions and assured him they wouldn't meet anymore sudden snowstorms before they arrived at Castiel despite the look of the heavy lowering clouds. He'd told them the one they met would come and he told them it would be of short duration. There would be no more for two days, then a few small flurries.

Z went back inside. No one had been surprised that he was alive and well and no one was surprised when they found Kak was dead – so one or more of them was a very good actor.

The rest of the day was uneventful. The unit got together to complete the map near the castle. The snow was beginning to melt away from ground heat, though the air was cold. He couldn't get away from them long enough to call Maita until after evemeal. He went outside and up onto the wall ramp just after dark with the golems tagging along. He used the com on their floater.

"Maita? You couldn't find which one of them sent Kak after me?" he asked.

I only had the golems and a com sender in Kad's office. I believe our villain knows better than to talk when the golems are about. That would be expected from the first. We can't hope to depend on them for that close a surveillance. I didn't tell you more at the first because, though I did watch Kak leaving and figured he was sent to do something, I wanted you to appear to be the great warrior from Dinkard. The golems had orders to see you or your men weren't harmed.

"The golems handled that part exactly right. I suppose you were directing them at the time," Z said. "So! How are our intrepid crew members doing with their own little projects?"

Well, I hope. I don't have much contact. T Six and TR say Kit and Tab are as puzzled with their job as we are with ours. Kurk and Thing aren't even in this plane so I don't know what's going on there except Thing must have given them some kind of power generation idea that's giving Tlorg a lot more free power than they'll ever be able to use at the same time. I've got whole sections of myself laid out for overhaul and have finished some other parts.

"But ... isn't that interplanal energy exchange supposed to be too dangerous to use?" Z asked.

I think the math's different enough there that it's safe. We both know Thing would never take any chances with that sort of thing. It will know positively if it's safe before it will even hint at using a thing.

"Well, I guess we'll just rock along here for now until we discover something we can grab onto," Z said. "I like the people a lot. They're a lot like the people on Earth except they aren't so violent."

They chatted about fifteen minutes, then Z went back down to his quarters for the night.

"Take the targets apart in that area and bring them closer over there," Z directed the next morning as they prepared the practice course. "If they're all the same distance apart you'll never be able to do anything with it. An enemy isn't going to space its troops out for you. Raise those hurdles a few centimeters higher. We don't want something the kirts can step over. You have to train the mounts to jump smoothly. If they pause as you come to an obstacle you lose your aim.

"Eil, get some of that brush away from the water hazards. We can put it back after the kirts learn to trust you riding them. We'll want them to be able to see what we're asking of them at first. If you understand and trust them they'll understand and trust you.

"We'll all have to work on the skin hangings over the wall after we get this part of the course finished. We can place the targets up there in a way I'll show you. It's not going to be easy, I promise! Remember! The enemy will have the wall to duck behind so you have to be quick.

"I know you don't know what I'm talking about. You won't for a halfyear at best, but I think better talking out loud. Let's get this done and I'll do a quick runthrough of the course and you'll see what you're going to be able to do before very long. I think I've seen enough about how you handle the kirts on our little trip out so I don't have doubts about any of that."

He kept the chatter and orders going for hours, moving at a steady pace to get it all ready, then rode the course, firing with stunning accuracy as he went. (Maita made him a bit of performance enhancer with the shield floater.) The men were impressed, as were several other guards along the upper fort walls. Captain Kad came to say he was as impressed with Z as he'd been with the guards at the festival in Castiel. What he was able to do was nothing short of astonishing!

"It's only a small part of what I'll teach the men here," Z promised. "We'll have one immediate advantage over the units in Castiel in that I'll be able to teach you some of the little tricks you need to know when there's snow on the ground.

"Remember one thing starting right now. When it's cold your bow is more brittle and if there's any water on your string it'll break easily. I'll show you a couple of tricks about that."

"You rubs lard-fat inter the string fer cold weather," Jok said. "The string won't take no water then and won't break so easy."

"That can work sometimes," Z agreed. "You do that when you don't have any light wax."

"Yup!" Jok said. "I kin see that! If'n you melts the wax in it won't soak off like lard!"

They got into a discussion of such tricks while they wiped down their kirts and fed them, then went in to evemeal telling stories of their younger years, those stories tending a bit to the bawdy. Z was glad they accepted him into that kind of close camaraderie so easily. He noticed they also included Captain Kad in the sessions. He liked that because it told him his instincts about Kad had been on the mark.

The following morning he started them all riding the practice course with their knees at the proper angle in the morning, then began the training of slipping the bow off the shoulder while fluidly taking the first arrow and inserting the bowstring at the same time. His own demonstrations had shown how important that could be and Kad's approval of their quick progress added a lot of interest on its own. They had all heard how the stipend for the units in Castiel had been doubled when the king noted how well they were performing.

The kirts at the fort weren't so easy to manage as the ones at Castiel. They hadn't known the intense training of the city-bred animals because these guards had too many other duties to spend the time with the animals, but that was soon taken care of and the program delay wasn't serious. Z was able to talk with Maita each evening, having slowly established the habit of going to the wall to relax watching the sunsets. The golems were seen all around the place at odd times and were soon ignored unless someone wanted the fun of matching insults and snide remarks with No. Neither they nor the hidden pickup in Kad's offices learned anything. It was going to be a slow process, but the time could well be used to teach the unit the skills that could someday become the basis for worldwide games of competition. Nothing really happened much out of the ordinary until the spring festival.

You're not going to be able to talk any longer. The unit's getting nervous about you riding this far away and apparently talking to yourself. You'll be in Castiel in a few minutes so we've covered about all of it. I haven't learned anything since you left. You know everything the golems learned in their little trips. I've almost completed my own renovation. You'll like some of the new things I've added. The guys are not sending emergency messages so they're fine. TAR One is doing better than I would have projected running things. There have been several Plutons who came to Tlorg through the portal according to the recorder there. They brought some things that they took back or at least they took the exact same weights of ... I'll be damned! That's how Thing did it! It will set up a ... I'm somewhat surprised that Thing – no I'm not. It's capable.

"What? The power thing?" Z asked.

Yes. You studied the spheres so you can see how the reversal of flow at the confluence would induce a secondary flow in a coil when the primary is inside. The primary would self-sustain as the balance equations cycled – or sequenced would be more exact – to produce a surplus. It's a part of abstract math that Thing talked with me about, so you probably couldn't understand it. I'm not sure I do.

"Right," Z replied. "I'll be able to see if they've kept up with the training of the units in Castiel or extended it in any way through how they perform at the games."

They were just coming in sight of Castiel and could see the bright banners announcing the games for the following day. It was a clear day with a lingering touch of frost in the air, but would be crisp and pleasant the day of the games and for several days thereafter, then the last cold front would move through bringing light snow flurries. Sto and Kad rode over to ask him if he was having any fun arguing with the golems. He'd as much as forgotten them while he and Maita used their floater com for com-munications, it being somewhat better than his shield set because he'd look strange holding the shield up for that long.

–We weren't arguing, Gangrene Brain! We were discussing the games and I was telling Turtle Face you came all this way just to be embarrassed by his former students. They've been practicing – you can wager on that!–

+Now, No! You know *perfect*ly well that Zho and this group have been practicing every chance they get! The competition is merely an excuse to get together outdoors where people can enjoy this de*light*ful weather! It's cool enough to be stimulating, yet warm enough to be comfortable. The warmth of the sunlight contrasted with the coolness of the breezes makes for a feeling of....+

–Just *per*fect weather to leave these living types with the sneezy-sniffles, Lichen Lips! Knock it the hells off with the delightful weather reports! What the hells do we care if it's just de*light*fully cool or colder than High Mountain? We're cast *metal* you halfassed moron!–

"You two both knock it off with the cute repartee," Z suggested. "It'll be fun to see what they've managed to teach themselves while we've been away. I don't doubt they'll have some surprises for us in the games.

"Isn't that Tor and Viz coming?"

The two riders came racing out to clap Z on the shoulder and welcome the unit to the games. They were to escort them to the special quarters they would use while in Castiel. It appeared they were to be housed separately from the other guards.

–You clown clones mean to tell us we ain't staying in the barracks? *One* thing will happen right!–

+Now, No! We wouldn't stay in the barracks in any case so why not put a more positive face on the chance of comradery we can share with our *dear* friends in....+

–YEEEEEE!–

"You're to stay in the palace as guests of King Fonz," Tor said. "I think he wants to argue with the golems. He gets some kind of fun out of that. I guess it gets boring sitting around in there all the time.

"It's good to see you again, Zho. We're trying to keep up with the skills and have even learned one or two things on our own, but it's not the kind of thing that seems to make Gyr or Nake happy. It's only stuff that looks good for the games and they want us to learn war things. Without someone like you to teach us things we can't do very much. I'd say how tired we get of all that kind of constant pushing, but that might not be much appreciated by others."

"We've learned to be big-eyed and enthusiastic when Nake or his friends are about and to go our own way when they're not," Kad agreed. "It wouldn't make them exactly ecstatic to learn that either if you see the way the stream flows.

"They're a necessary type in politics, but things would be far better for everyone if they were all to retire or something."

"I think we're going to get on pretty well," Viz said. "Be very careful what you say to anyone not on the team. *Any*one!"

That seemed a rather strange kind of warning to Z, but he would wait. He was there to learn. He still didn't know who it was he was against except in a general sense. He certainly wouldn't waste time trying not to offend such as Gyr and Nate. So far it had worked pretty much the way he'd planned.

–Has Barrel Butt put on much more weight since we were here? I think he's headed for trouble if he doesn't watch it!

He can barely get in the door now! It's a good thing the kirts don't have to carry him!–

"Nake seems to find ways to add a kilo here and there," Tor agreed with a grin. "For someone who's so determined to have all us guards in such perfect physical condition he really sets a great example!

"Gyr's put on a little, but he has sense enough to try to get it back off again. I think he worries about how he looks in the uniform. They're neat when they fit right, but the women are turned away by that wobble hanging out front."

+Speaking of Nake and Gyr, they're waiting to greet us right over there! How truly considerate! A hearty welcoming committee – well, Nake's a committee all by himself, but it was nice of Gyr to come along, don't you think?

+I feel sorry for the poor kirts who have to pull a carriage with the ever-expanding Nake in it! I'm amazed that the wheelhubs don't freeze and refuse to turn. He describes the meaning of the saying 'the pebble that breaks the axle' – though I have to admit in Nake's case it's the boulder that breaks the entire carriage. I never cease to wonder how anyone....+

–GHAK! The pebble that's your brain couldn't break an eightleg webber's strand!–

They rode up to dismount in front of Gyr and Nake, who were almost formal in their manner until Yan and Wil strolled out to embrace Z and to ask how things were going in the Hill Fort. The officers seemed not to like the closeness of the guards and this barbarian at all! Nake in particular decided he didn't care to challenge Zho de Dinkard so didn't say anything.

–Hey, Bat Brains! How have things been here in the civilized parts of the kingdom? Have you managed to forget everything Zho taught you yet?–

"We try, but remembrances keep slipping in!" Yan shot back with a smirk. "Forgetfulness takes practice – as you obviously know!"

+It is so good to see our friends again! I see you are keeping quite fit and well. Perhaps it would be well advised that your superior officers take a lesson or two from *you*!

+I hear King Fonz wishes to match wits with No again. Poor No will be so far out of practice himself that I just know we're going to be horribly embarrassed! No needs to have a constant challenge or he gets a *lit*tle bit, shall we say, rusty with his delivery timing. I think perhaps if....+

–I don't think you think! Who the hells asked you, Bug Brain? King Fonz is one of the few people I've met who can handle any intelligent conversation. It's a refreshing change from the ordinary types.

–We'll float over to the castle and see the king.–

+Oh, let's stay out here where the air is so refreshing and crisp! We can overlook such as Nake for this kind of beaUTiful weather. The sun is in the sky and the breeze teasing at our hair! The green green grass is peeking through....+

–AHHHH, SHUT UP, Bone Brain! Why do you always have to come across with that gooey poetry crap? Why can't you just *once* act like you had something other than bronze in that ugly dome you call your head? Where in the nine hells is all that damned *hair* you're blathering about? A damned typhoon would be a *breeze* to *us*! SHEESH!–

The floater drifted toward the castle while the group shook their heads at one another and grinned.

+But, No! Bronze is all that *either* of us has in our heads!+ Yes was saying as they drifted off. +You must try to remember that Kant cast us with only the very *finest* bronze and spent *hours* making the molds just right so we'd....+

–AAAAHHH, SHUT THE HELLS UP!–

"You've had to listen to that crap all winter?" Gyr asked, staring at the floater. "It's a good thing you were stationed way out there! I'd be driven mad by now!"

"We like them!" Kad said. "After awhile you learn how to keep them from interfering with you. Don't react to them and they'll drift away. After a few days you don't even know when they're around you anymore. They serve their own purpose because you hear both sides of any problem argued. They're really a lot of fun.

"Well? Where are we to stay? I want to go to the lake and get some of this road dust off of me!"

Lest came across the courtyard to greet them and Z strolled off with him toward the inn. Nake obviously didn't like that and Gyr seemed about to protest, but they kept their silence.

"Did you ever find that fellow who was missing when we left the fort?" Lest asked as they walked along. "Was I shown to be right? He's dead?"

"I suppose he must be," Z replied. "He never came back and we had some vicious weather a couple of days later. His kirt came back without him, as you already know, so he most probably died of exposure somewhere in the mountains.

"I didn't know him. He may be a mountain man and still be around somewhere, but I doubt it. I've been in those mountains and there really isn't anywhere a person could stay for the whole winter or even a few tendays. There's not enough food after the snows run it all into the caves or valleys."

Lest laughed and said he meant to ask if they'd found the body. There was no doubt the subject was already dead when the burning test was applied. That test never failed.

They talked for more than an hour more over cav and sweetcakes at the inn, then Z went to the castle to be shown to his quarters, which were more than comfortable. The rest of his unit were in the courtyard bathing pool, so he joined them. The evening was uneventful other than the feeling of being constantly watched from some point just outside of his line of vision. He'd had that feeling before and was puzzled by it. If there were any electronic surveil-lance devices around the spy floater would surely detect them easily.

The feelings were generally from his body's keen ability to detect small unusual emanations in the electromagnetic spectrum. Maita enhanced the ability many years ago.

He'd have to remember to be extremely careful when and where he communicated with Maita. He knew enough about his "feelings" to know there was a reason for his uneasiness.

Put the micro-receiver directly inside your ear and direct answers to the golems. Code what you want to say so it will seem natural, came quietly from the shield as he rode around the course of the games alone the following morning. The golems were above him making their usual comments.

–The kirt course isn't really bad at all, Algae Brain!– No remarked brightly (For it). –I think there will be some real added challenges. They could certainly use some decent challenges to break them out of their usual stone lazy mode! Action, at last!–

+It's a perfectly *love*ly clean field, it's in absolutely *won*derful condition and the weather is just about *per*fect! I think the teams will have a lot of fun with this and the people will find the diversions of the games to greatly brighten the coming of the de*light*ful spring breezes! Everything is so clean and *bright*!+

"You know something? You're even beginning to get to me with that nicey-nice crap," Z replied. "I wonder if that stand over there is strong enough to hold Nake, Gyr, Fonz and the rest of that bunch. Nake seems to have gotten a hell of a lot bigger – in a lot of directions – than when we were here before.

"Gyr seems to listen to what we say more than before, too. He hears a lot more than he's letting on. I've caught the way he can look a bit toward one side and seem to be concentrating on something else, but his body language tells me he's listening.

"I wonder if he's telling it to Fonz, Nake or others."

–Probably tells everything he knows or guesses to Knuckle Nose. That one seems to be getting much too large for a stand that size to support!–

Nake does seem to have more power, but he still has enough sense to defer to Gyr and has some fear of Lest I believe. I don't know where his support's coming from. He doesn't have the intelligence to be behind any of this unless he's a lot better actor than I have any reason to believe. There's a connection somewhere to other things and through someone who we are either not considering or who we don't know about.

"Putting those targets over there by the stands wasn't very smart," Z said. "The king or any of the people there could get hurt if anyone were to miss. It seems a very dangerous way to do things. It seems much too good an opportunity for an accident. I'll tell Gyr about it. Maybe he let the others place the targets and will suggest they move them."

–Who the nine hells cares if the damned whole bunch of them get shot? Maybe the best thing would be for them all to have a fatal accident, then the people could take over themselves! This whole guard thing is silly! Why not go for the easy way out for once in your sordid life?–

*The talk around town seems to be starting to turn somewhat against King Fonz. I can't find where it started, but there's now a definite undercurrent. Maybe you'd better try to find a way to protect Fonz. He could be our most valuable ally in this later and the fact the people are slowly being directed away from him indicates he's *not* the one behind any of it. He is somehow being vilified while being kept unaware of it if you know what I'm trying to say.*

"Oh, I think the king's not so bad – as politicians go," Z said. "I wouldn't care if Nake got a stray arrow through the throat. An arrow couldn't penetrate all that fat to get him in the body. He's really getting to be gross – that's an expression from another place. Where I was born.

"I think we'll win in this game, but it's going to be a lot closer than I thought at first. They might well be depending on someone we don't know about. Some of those competitors from the countryside were very good the first time we had the games and they'll have improved since last fall."

We still don't know who's behind it, but don't forget the warning from Viz. I think he knows who really runs things here and was trying to warn you. He has to be careful because he's not in a position for you to protect him from them and I think the men here definitely look to you as a protector.

+I think the weather will be just *beautiful* for the games, don't you? The townsfolk and the farm gentry will be *so* pleased to be able to congregate together here for this *won*derful little festival! They can converse and trade news of what has happened to their own families over the winter.

+I wonder how many will come from out of town? I wonder if the better players in the skill games will be from inside the city of Castiel at all. These things are so much fun if one doesn't know exactly where the competition really lies! There is the thrill of the unknown in a way to add to the excitement of....+

–Look, Mold Mind, that's exactly Zho's point! Those targets over there aren't placed like the ones the country people will practice on. They could very easily shoot a few arrows through Fonz, which would deprive me of all intelligent conversation. I would think some of those country ignoramuses would be very likely to do exactly that. It wouldn't be one of the trained guardsmen because Zho has always impressed on them that they have to be able to choose their target and wouldn't miss to where an arrow could go into the stand.–

"We really will have to see that King Fonz is protected," Z said. "There's not much danger from the farmers because few of them are part of the archery tests. The danger's probably from our own ranks. The danger's where the shot's bounced from the target from a near-miss. That's the one that could go into the stands.

"Why am I arguing with you? I'll simply tell Gyr to have the targets moved a few meters toward one side and the problem's solved.

"It's like coming home to find that *things* are changed just a little bit. I hope the *kurks* are all in good shape. I want to catch up with the news around here and sort of keep *tabs* on how much has changed.

"Where's the repair *kit*? Is it complete and back where it belongs?"

You don't make any sense, but people who argue with those golems never do. Thing and Kurk are back on EC. It seems they had quite the little vacation on Hades and Thing was able to somehow completely change the way Hades does things and even to get them working on building their own little empire. Tab and Kit have almost solved their own problems and will finish soon and return to EC. TR and T Six are a bit bored. They're keeping a lookout on some strange things that are happening. It seems there's a rumor starting that the Maitan Empire's beginning to crumble. They're busy planning our next little adventure, I think. My new abilities detected the first of the rumors and located the likely points of origin. It's odd, but not too dangerous. You're about to have company.

Lest was riding along with Gyr and was rapidly approaching so things would have to get back to normal.

–Well! If it isn't good old Push Puss and Muck Mouth!– No greeted brightly as Gyr and Lest rode up. –Out here to see if you can find a way to kill off the king and his advisors?–

+Now, No! Be nice! Lest will be right there with Fonz and so will Gyr. I'm sure they don't care to place themselves into a position of danger like that. Only Nake is so stupid as to place those targets in such a manner! One sees his handiwork in any of the myriad idiocies around Castiel, as usual. It is such a nice day outside I think you should leave the negativism inside. Everyone should remain happy and carefree on such an invigorating day, don't you agree?+

"For No, that *is* a positive attitude!" Z shot back quickly. "How are things, Gyr? Lest?

"No's right, I believe. Those four targets should be moved more toward one side or another. If anyone slips as he fires he could shoot right into the king's stand. An arrow on the edge of the outer targets could deflect right at the box."

"Great hopping flidgets! You're right!" Gyr cried with a strange greatly surprised and almost frightened look. "I'll have the targets moved immediately! That is something we cannot allow!

"I told Lest your approval of the course was critical. I've never denied for an instant that you know far more than do any of us what could happen with these weapons. I would never have thought of the chance of such an accident! I'll handle it right now.

"This is *terribly* distressing! How could such an over-sight have happened?!"

He rode off toward the kirt stalls calling for Tor to order the men to move those targets by the king's box. Now! And to see that such thoughtless and ill-considered things didn't happen again.

"Hmm. Very astute," Lest noted. "I wonder if you think perhaps someone *wants* to remove the king or myself – or maybe Nake and Gyr?"

"I heard a couple negative comments at the inn last night," Z said. "I didn't hear anything at all against King Fonz when I was here before, but now it seems there's some kind of an odd tension building up. You probably wouldn't be aware of it. You're in the middle of the whole mess all the time and the change is gradual. I've seen this sort of thing before and know it can get nasty.

"I personally wonder where it's coming from. I don't know of one single thing Fonz has done that would call for what I've heard."

*What are you *doing*?!* came from the little radio receiver in his ear.

"You've overheard something in the inn?" Lest asked, showing a little surprise. "I usually hear anything long before any.... I don't remember hearing anything in the inn other than normal conversation."

"It's subtle. It's more a slant in the direction of the conversation than in anything that's said directly. There was a negative addition to it that wasn't there in the fall. There's a little bit of dissatisfaction in the way people are looking at things, a discontent even the people don't know the cause of. There isn't any reason for it! It's the kind of thing that people who study the way people are influenced on a secondary level of the mind are steered by.

"I've seen this crap before. It was the same kind of thing

back in Kornwhich and Judolph. The people slowly get worked up over a long period of time by someone who wants to take over the area. It's a very deliberate thing. Even from the first you questioned why anyone would want a guard trained in what is very obviously *not* a defensive posture. This is probably part of the same thing.

"It always results in disaster. The person behind this is no different than Hooch de Judolph or Tyj de Kornwhich. They wanted to get some kind of personal power, started this exact same kind of thing and ended up reviled and despised by their people. Unfortunately a lot of those people were killed before it was over.

"I wonder who's behind this. I think whoever it is will be greatly surprised when they learn what I've taught the men! That knowledge will come a little too late to be of any use to them, I will promise you! There's a lot more to this than either of us knows right now, but this isn't some new and great idea. Not even maybe! This is as old as the history of Gaerkt itself. It's only the arrogance of the insane that makes the one who plans it fail to see he's no different than ten thousand others. He probably thinks he's come up with some great plot no one's ever thought of before.

"I see the king's arrived. It's almost time for the games to begin."

Viz and Tor rode out to move the targets, Z rode toward the king's box to greet Fonz and Lest sat leaning forward a bit in his saddle to stare at Z's back with a thoughtful expression on his face.

What was that about? What have you learned? Will Lest be able to put an end to it? came from Z's ear.

"Oh, I think he can put a quick end to it," Z mumbled. "The question is, will he?"

"We will appreciate your running the course as you did

last meet," King Fonz said to Z after the units had finished their competitions. "There is a good balance between the two camps, each having won two firsts of the major competitions. The individual arts were split fairly well among all contestants and the open competitions were won by normal citizens as well as by the two guard units – which is as it should be. Such a close balance of skills is to the advantage of all citizens. Lest and I have agreed to award no further points for your competition, but to time you and compare your accuracy to that of your students. We have a little wager between us as to whether any of your students have surpassed your own skills."

–King Bird Lips here has bet you'll still beat them all and Bone Brain bets they beat you because they've been practicing while you've been laying around on your tender sweet ass! I personally am forced to agree with the local magic practitioner because he's in a position to forecast.–

+Now, No! You know perfectly well that these skills are so learned by Zho that he'll make a mockery of the others! Lest hasn't forecast any of it because he likes the bet to be based on things outside his control. If you would simply allow the....+

–I'll *allow* you to shut the hells up!–

So. Lest thought he had some sort of control over Z's ability to compete, did he? What was going on here? Was he right in what he suddenly suspected?

I've had the golems directly behind them for the past half hour and they didn't even know it, came in his ear. *I think Lest will offer you something to drink from the red wine goblet under his seat. He put something in it. *What* is going on?*

"I'll be honored to run the full course if you'll find it entertaining," Z answered. "I would like to know if my skills deteriorated any over the winter. It isn't easy to practice in the snow. On the other shoulder for balance I have been concentrating on other things that may prove valuable."

"Shall we all enjoy a bit of this excellent wine King Fonz was kind enough to supply while the announcement is made?" Lest asked. "It is mild and will not interfere with your skills, I think."

Put a drop on the analyzer.

"Thank you," Z replied, taking the goblet Lest held out to him, managing to spill a couple of drops on his shield as his kirt reacted to an "accidental" bump by his foot. "Perhaps a short toast to the festival games and to the dedication of the guards to learning their skills well."

King Fonz stood to hold up his own goblet high and announce loudly, "To the good health and happiness of the wonderful athletes who have here competed today! May your rewards be multiplied and may contentment and peace be upon all our houses!"

It contains a mild organic hallucinogen. Take the pill on the shield as you begin your run and I'll manage to augment your performance enough to surprise even Lest. I don't know if this was supposed to help or hinder you. You have to tell me what's really going on when this is over! I've very obviously missed something – or is it one of your hunches?

Z raised up in his saddle and drained the goblet, set it in the edge of the platform and rode to the start of the course, taking the pill as soon as his back was to the stand. He'd had some experience with the enhancers Maita could produce before and was almost immediately flushed with a distorted time sense. He expected it and wasn't worried. Everything was now moving at what seemed a very slowed pace to him and all his senses were heightened. He rode the course much faster than any of the other competitors and felt he had more than enough time to compensate for every least little movement of the kirt. Where he would normally have to move the arrow across the target and fire as he crossed the proper point he had time to take far more careful aim. That coupled with the skill of the person the crystal was made from made every shot strike very near the center of the expert circle. He returned to the stand to wild cheers from the men of both his old units from Castiel and his new one from the fort. King Fonz was purely ecstatic and Lest was as purely unbelieving. The enhancer wore off within a few more seconds, letting him drift back to normal very quickly. Maita could time the effects of the chemicals to within a few seconds.

"That was amazing!" Fonz declared. "I didn't think it was possible for the course to be run so fast – *or* so accurately! You were a blur! You were amazing! I've never seen anything like it!"

–Yeah, Snake Snoot! You cost me half the winnings I'd saved up! I bet against you! Thanks heaps! How come you all of a sudden got so good at this crap? Have you been holding out on me?–

"I really don't know," Z replied in a bewildered tone. "I was starting the course and everything seemed to slow down. It was as if the kirt was barely dragging along at first and that my time was going to be poor. Sounds became extremely low in tone and everyone was moving like in a dream, like they were purposely moving at less than half normal speed! I seemed to be watching it all from somewhere off to the side!

"The same thing happened once before. It was at a party in Horgland. The sorcerer put some kind of powder in the beer and the same kind of thing happened to me. It put most of the others to sleep and a couple of them went sort of nutzo, but it was fun.

"I wonder if it was the wine? Did it do anything like that

to either of you? Maybe it was spoiled or something?"

"Not to me!" Fonz protested. "It was the same wine we've all been drinking all day. Lest poured it for all of us at the same time."

"No," Lest answered. "I feel perfectly normal except for being more than a bit in awe of your performance. I don't see how it could have anything to do with the wine we all drank. Perhaps you ate or drank something earlier that had any number of things in it. Some of the poisons in plants can cause such a reaction.

"I know the powder your magic man used in Horgland. It can have greatly different reactions than he planned because.... It does that."

"I always chew on sweetgrass stems while I'm watching the guys practice," Z said. "Maybe I picked up the wrong one and didn't notice.

"I will say one thing! I wish I knew what it was! It would really be something to give to the guards if they ever had to fight a real battle!"

"It affects different people in different ways, as you've noted," Lest warned. "It can as easily slow you down as speed you up. It can also put you to sleep or drive you into a kind of insanity for awhile. Its effects on nine of ten people tend to the negative."

"Well, I wish I knew what it was, anyway," Z insisted. "It sure doesn't slow *me* down!"

The rest of the day was uneventful except for when the head of an ax came off during the throws. The heavy hardened bronze ax missed Nake by mere centimeters. It would have hit him squarely in the face if he hadn't reached down to pick up a large platter of sweetbread at just that moment.

Nake was to have been the target? It didn't make any sense anymore. Nake was necessary to the plan if it was at all like

Z thought.

Z noted the farmer who was making the throw and saw he was shaken by the accident. It wasn't a planned thing on his part. Period. Gyr seemed far more upset than Nake, who said he always had phenomenal luck anyhow and no harm done. They'd know to hold all future competitions where that sort of thing couldn't happen.

That more or less solidified what Z suspected, but the attempt on Nake still didn't make sense. He had missed something.

The evening was spent with all the competitors at the palace dining hall, then the unit got some rest for the long trip back to the fort the following day.

You think Lest is involved. Anyone can see that. I'll ask why when we have time to talk. I was surprised at Gyr's reaction to that axe. Nake seemed almost smug. There's more to this than we thought. We're looking in all the wrong places, I think. I think we're being deliberately led to look in the wrong places.

They were riding toward the hill fort. It was cool and a bit foggy on the road so early, but would clear soon.

Z couldn't answer, but Maita was mostly thinking through the whole operation so Z could consider its points and refute them later.

–Hey-ho! Bedsore Butt!– No called, floating above from ahead. –There seems to be a bit of an obstruction across the road about two kilometers ahead. A stream decided to change course and wash it out, all by itself! Isn't that odd?!–

+Now, No! You know we went along the stream to find the bank had washed out and changed its path! It's such a delightful crisp day why don't we detour to the south a few hundred meters ahead where we can avoid the washout altogether? We can ride through the meadows and across the old farmers' road back to the fort road and only take a few minutes more for the trip and those moments will be spent in a truly de*light*ful jaunt through colorful pastoral and picturesque fields of early season flowers! Now, wouldn't that be much better than getting all upset for nothing? If you look for the negative side of things all the time they will find you! If you look for the positive....+

–AHHH, STICK IT IN YOUR UGLY NOSE! You've got some serious gangrene of the brain – except you ain't got no brains to get gangrene in! It didn't occur to you we can float off anywhere we want? We ain't riding no smelly kirt in case it didn't penetrate the lead in your head!–

+I merely suggested those who *are* riding kirts could simply avoid a lot of hard work and inconvenience while enjoying the beauty and serenity of the countryside.

+As to the odor of the kirts, I'll quote you in saying, 'in case it didn't register on what passes for your mind we're cast *bronze*! We don't *smell* anything!'

+I'm sorry. I shouldn't allow your negative attitude to get to me like that, No, but *why* must you always jump to such negative conclusions about everything? Look for the brightness at the edge, the sun shines bright on the meadows of the....+

–ZHEEEEE! I CAN'T STAND MUCH MORE OF THIS!–

The golems soon floated off ahead, No almost sobbing and pleading for Yes to –SHUT THE HELLS UP, BUTTFACE!–

"Well? Is Yes right?" Kad asked. "Would it be easier if we went around through the farm road?"

"Why not?" Z replied. "It's not much farther and we don't have to go through that stream if it's as cold as I think it will be this time of year. The kirts will appreciate not being asked to ford the stream."

"It's the snow melt that made it get so high it washed the bank our, probably," Eil suggested. "It'll be awful cold. I agree to that."

"Then we go around by the farm road," Z announced.

They rode to the cutoff and along as the day cleared and the fog lifted. There weren't any more problems.

The washout was caused by felling a large tree across the stream and gouging out a little place for the water to go over the bank a bit farther back so it would wash and run down that little ditch. There were four men waiting by the stream where it crossed the road. They were con-cealed in the forest nearby and had crossbows. They would wait until you were in the cold water to attack while your defenses were down and you were slowed by the cold water. It was about as well thought out as the other things they've done. The kirts would be in the water and you wouldn't have been affected much, only slowed down a little.

Z was riding around the fort checking his regular route. It was late in the day and they had returned from Castiel only two hours past.

"I wonder if it was only me they were trying to kill?" Z mumbled.

Probably. Are you still feeling you're being watched and listened to?

"No. Just the normal precautions while we're this close to anyone," Z replied. "I think I have to be fairly close to Lest for him to use the powers to listen to me."

That was the hunch you had? That he was using one of those spells to watch you?

"That was all it could be," Z agreed. "They don't have any technology so no electronics so no transmitting microphones. Once I decided on that the rest sort of fell into place. The only problem as I now see it is that we don't know if he's been acting for someone else. The attempt on

Nake puts us right back to a point where we can't figure the whole pattern."

What was the old pattern and why don't you think it might have changed?

"The old pattern was pretty much what I told Lest had happened in those two places I made up," Z replied. "I wanted to see his reaction. It would show me if he was a leader in the scheme or if he was working for someone else.

"I never thought Fonz was any part of it and I still don't. The way it looks now is that Nake's the head of it and everyone else is doing whatever he orders. Lest is going along with it for reasons of his own and it worries me that I can't figure what they could be. He's definitely not interested in power. I think I showed Lest what Nake has in mind. That farmer didn't plan to throw any axe at Nake. That was done right there and then. Only Lest could have done it.

"Why was Nake so unconcerned about it? It was very obvious someone tried to kill him.

"Why was Gyr so upset? He's only a dupe and doesn't have any idea what's going on.

"Why did Lest try to kill Nake? Was it only meant as a strong warning of some kind? If it was like I thought, a power-grabbing scheme such as I described, nothing else quite fits. I still find it very hard to believe Nake has enough intelligence to think of anything such. It's equally hard to believe Gyr would think of it, but why his reactions if he's not head of the mess?"

Because it's Lest all along. You just don't want to admit it. You like him.

"Then why the attempt on *me* today?" Z asked. "That doesn't make any sense! The things I'm training these men to do are the only chance the scheme would have to succeed and Lest damned well knows it! Why would he be starting rumors against Fonz? He would need Fonz to keep the thing together. No Fonz would mean the people would fragment in their support of anyone else and the guard would be the first thing to disband. It was the idea of *Fonz* to have a large guard to employ people who couldn't find gainful work elsewhere. Someone *else* moved in on that to start this plan of taking over things.

"No matter what, none of it makes any damned sense!"

–Hey, Fog Brain! It makes perfect sense! It makes the same kind of sense Yes and I make!–

"What?" Z said, startled.

+No is right. The reason such a plan wouldn't work in the ways you described in your fictional accounts of Kornwhich and Judolph is because a target would be presented to attack. If you attack No you aid me. If you attack me you aid No. If you attack Nake you aid Lest. If you attack Lest you aid Nake.+

And Lest contrived an attack on Nake, thus aiding himself – after you pointed out to him that the scheme wasn't anything new.

"While Nake arranged the attack on me on the way back here because he thinks he's really in charge of this whole plot," Z said. "He's scared of me because I rode that course so fast and was so accurate. He fears what I might be teaching these men here because there's no way he could control them if they have those abilities."

Lest started the rumors against Fonz. He could then present himself as an alternative to Nake if Fonz were deposed because he's well-respected around Castiel while Nake is not liked at all. That would tend to determine who actually ended up with power.

"The attempt on me shows we've had quite an effect on pretty much everyone," Z agreed. "Nake's afraid of me and Lest knows I've figured him out. The whole thing's falling apart for both of them."

+What's Gyr so afraid of?+

"We have to find out what friend Gyr knows that's got him so damned afraid," Z decided. "I don't have the least idea of how to accomplish that little feat!"

*I think you can make the excuse that you must speak with King Fonz about the games and that it's your duty to report the damage to the road so the king can order repairs. You can ride into Castiel and can find time to get Gyr alone. I'll try to find a way to interfere with Lest's magic watching you. I can get some information from Tlorg about that (Book five: *Now You See It – Now You Don't*). We can settle this whole thing now. I don't think there's any real danger of it happening again if we can make it known widely enough that there WAS such a scheme and that it could have worked. If these people are aware of it they'll be able to protect themselves against it. You can become another sort of barbarian legend that the whole world will know about in their lore. That will stabilize what we've done for centuries.*

–Sheesh! Fish Face becomes a damned legend on still *another* world! He's contaminating the whole damned galaxy!–

"It's too late!" Z replied. "You've already shown that you can solve logic problems! Thanks for the solution to this little dilemma.

–*Little* dilemma?! You were blopping around like a wounded flitterbug! You'd never have solved the mess and neither would the Great Emperor Platinum Pate!–

+Now, No! It's part of our purpose to aid in solving these puzzles. When we work together we do great things. Pull apart and smallness brings!+

–YEEEEEEEEE!–

Back to normal!

<u>*Assassinated!*</u>

"I'm going out as early as I can manage, Kad," Z reported next morning before dawnmeal. "I want to discuss several things with Nake and Gyr and I want to tell King Fonz how the course for the games can be improved and about the washout in the road so he can order it be fixed. I'm sure he expects that kind of thing to be reported anytime any of us know about it.

"The unit can practice the hurdles and jumps. I wasn't very happy with the way Viz and Tor were able to beat us at that. They didn't have the problems we have up here so they were able to practice a lot more, but we should never make excuses. If we make excuses we'll get lazy. We'll have to work on that until it's right.

"Lest said there would be a couple of small flurries, then we'll have spring. We can set up our mountain course so I can start on a few of those things when I get back. The training's nowhere near complete without that.

"I hope to be no more than today to handle everything. I'll stay overnight in Castiel and be back here tomorrow before midmeal."

"You might discuss some ways to design the next course a bit better," Kad suggested. "There were a few times I worried about accidents. That little axe-throw near-miss with Nake should make him willing to listen."

–Why the hells do you think we're going at all, Gnat Brain? Snarkle Snout already *said* he wanted to discuss the course with Lard Butt and the king of nuthin'! Don't you even listen to what *you* say?–

+Now, No! Kad was merely reminding Zho to be sure to mention spectator safety! A tragedy that is so easily avoided could well ruin the games permanently. It's certainly a beautiful day for a little trip, don't you think? It's so clean and *bright* during this time of the year! The weather's nearly perfect for a leisurely little ride into the countryside! Castiel should be just *lovely* now!+

—I'd like to leave you in Castiel, Pewter Puss! You could nice them all to death! You could croak casketworms with that nicey-nice crap!–

"Damn it all! I see you two have elected to come with me," Z said dejectedly. "Other than that I think it probably *will* be a nice trip."

They got out as quickly as they could before Kad thought up any reasons for them not to go. Z wanted to get to Gyr before anything happened that would make him too afraid to talk – and any hint he might say anything could be damned dangerous to him. Viz had known something, too, so he wanted a word alone with him. Maybe between the two of them he could resolve at least one of his questions.

It all came down to Lest. He had to be the one behind it by the simple process of elimination – but was there someone more powerful above him? Was it some kind of strange partnership in conspiracy?

Somehow Lest simply didn't seem the type to be doing it. Z didn't believe for one second Lest would try to have him killed and the explanation they worked out didn't hold up so well this morning. There was something more to it. Something was obvious and was very close, but just past being seen.

They were about six kilometers away from Castiel when the golems reported there was a lot of activity along a stretch of the road ahead near the river that was sure to be directed toward Z. Somehow they knew he was coming.

"I suppose they learned that with some kind of spell," Z replied. "There simply isn't any other way a message could be sent that fast here."

*You realize this ties your friend, Lest, right smack in the middle of it. They're setting a trap you can't possibly survive. They *know* you're coming!*

"Maybe I'd better let them be successful," Z suggested. "Is it something where they'll know definitely if I was killed?"

I'll work out something with some floaters. They'll be just a bit more successful than they'd hoped so they won't be able to ever retrieve your body. Zho de Dinkard will become a stronger legend if we can let it be known to all the people in Castiel and the fort that he was deliberately murdered.

"What about the golems?" Z asked. "I'd think they could be used to make that little fact one nobody could miss."

Yes. Something along those lines. I'll let them barely manage to escape and they can go on into Castiel to go on a rampage because of the killing. We'll see how our sorcerer reacts to the fact he can't do anything about them. What do you plan now?

"I think it's about time Mikill returned," Z answered. "He's supposed to have that little bit of power so the golems.... I will be absolutely and totally *damned*!"

What?

"Who did we forget about since right at the first in all of this mess?" Z asked. "Who was like the golems? Always there, always at the edge of consciousness? Who blended into the landscape to the point no one noticed if he was there or not?"

+Right! He sort of faded into the background after that little bit where Nake came into it! He was always around, then he suddenly wasn't anymore and no one noticed.+

–Uh-huh! Now which snaketurd among this bunch was the very first one Flob Face was worried might send him to the fort too early, but who never did anything more than be there for the threat?–

Mako!?

–Give Sluice Breath first trophy! I'm slipping! I saw him all over that damned castle all the time. He was always very overly interested in everything, then he suddenly wasn't around anymore and wasn't asking any questions. He was so secondary I didn't note it – and I pride myself in noting *everything!*–

+He was always there and was with Lest's wife a lot of the time, then he was with Nake a bit, then he drifted back to his duties and seemed to ignore all of us,+ Yes said musingly. +He was so unimpressive we forgot he existed! I wonder if he's one part of the whole thing or if he's the leader. He's the perfect hiderspider. He takes on the drabber colors around him and doesn't exhibit anything to catch at the attention of anyone.+

"It's certainly suspicious," Z said. "I was going to depend on using his daughter to have me sent out to the hill fort, but Nake beat him to it. I don't know how or why I was able to so quickly and completely forget about him!"

He was our major player, then even I let him slip out of my consciousness. If he's a close friend of Marla.... He could have Lest learn things that way. He might be a lot smarter than we guess. Maybe your sorcerer friend isn't involved nearly so much as I thought. I would think he could be manipulated by anyone who knows him well, and Mako could be using his wife for exactly that purpose. He could plan and direct from the shadows in a manner of speaking. He could appear to simply be another tree in the forest.

"It fits a lot better from that angle," Z agreed. "I believe Lest is no more than someone who's being used. You're right about that."

–You wish, Moss Brain! He'd have to be able to figure some things out and he'd have to be the one who did that thing with the axe flying at Nake's head. Don't forget the obvious!–

That's an oddity from any angle. I'll project what's now happening at the trap on the shield screen if you care to watch. You golems hurry up. You have to be high enough over Z to escape the trap.

Z slid the screen out of the rim of the shield and watched as a floater with a holovid projection of himself riding the kirt surrounding it "trotted" under a high ledge near the riverbank with the golems above making nasty remarks and sweet replies. There was a loud yelling and a large section of the ledge folded outward and fell to cover the floater, missing the golems by no more than a few dozen centimeters. No was screaming obscenities as they flew at one of the six men who had dislodged the bank, knocking him atop the pile of rubble.

I used a floater underground to drop off about ten times what they planned so they won't be able to dig your body out of it. I'll send the golems to Castiel to report the murder. You come on aboard to be changed back to Mikill complete with your medallion and a floater that has those electronic emanations for Lest to detect. It's probably best that you don't show up too immediately for coincidence. Lest is too intelligent to miss that so you can find some way to explain it.

"Late this afternoon," Z agreed. "Send the golems to report to the hill fort first, then they can come to Castiel to report to King Fonz and Lest tonight. I'll be at the inn with Lest when they come in so I can watch his reaction. If he's any part of it it will be obvious because he will be certain the golems can somehow learn who ordered the killing."

Maita sent a floater with a modification unit on it for Z to change the patch patterns on his kirt and to make it darker, then he freed the animal and climbed aboard the expanded shield to fly to Maita.

*You're Mikill again. I've told you some of what Thing and Kurk were doing. Kurk says Thing will *never* again go on another vacation with him! Thing seems to have caused a major revolution on Hades and some other world in that TTH plane. It was able to virtually take over two worlds somehow, but nothing Thing does surprises me. It was probably just relaxing and the whole thing was some kind of weird joke. I'm sure it wouldn't do anything that might actually cause harm to anyone. Tab and Kit and the ships are back on EC as of a few hours ago and are monitoring the new problem, but there's no hurry.*

"You said you were so happy they were all away on safe missions this time so you didn't have to worry!" Z said. "With Thing you should know better. It's too much like me."

Well, first Kit was ordered to kill Tab, then Tab was supposed to kill Kit so they really had some fun. Kurk and Thing had a good time, too. They always swear they'll never so much as go across a room with each other again, then they do! You can get all the details when we meet at your place again after we finish here. I don't think it'll be long now. My projects are all completed! I'm rather different in a lot of ways. TAR One is running the empire smoothly. TR and T Six are putting in some of the better modifications we invented while they wait for us. I've also improved the atomic architect and programed in that breadroot thing for you.

"I suppose I'd better get back to Castiel fairly soon," Z said. "Give me some information on where Mikill's supposed to have been for the past halfyear or so. I may have to talk about it and there may be ways to check – if they could find I was going to Castiel from the fort."

*You can explain part of it as being things various people taught you, then you can say you took a boat from Pfen

Point to the island of Glortherd where you took another boat to various other islands. You can secondary the crystal in the tray. It has all the information you could want about those islands. You can mention landmarks or such if anyone's ever been there.*

Z picked up the little crystal and put it into the socket, grinned, used the hand sealer on the earlobe and went to the cargo hold to get on his shield/floater. He headed for the river road a few hundred meters downstream from Castiel.

Castiel was peaceful and serene as he waved at the guard at the city gates and strolled on in to the inn to hire a room from Gild. Lest was at his customary side table with Marla and he waved at them, then remembered that Mikill never met Lest's wife so he went over to introduce himself to her and to ask Lest how things were going.

"A bit too smoothly, I fear," Lest replied. "Things have a definite habit of turning vicious when there's so long a period of serenity. I become apprehensive."

"Dear, you know perfectly well there is simply no reason to be so pessimistic!" Marla said jovially. "We are running in such a track and things are so everyday normal it seems placid. There are always things happening we know nothing about, so don't seek trouble and it won't so easily find you!"

"So! How is the philosophy proceeding?" Lest asked. "Have you found the time to study the patterned movements of the firmament in your wanderings?"

"I have enough trouble deciding where *I'm* going, much less the stars!" Z replied. "Have you found anything new?"

"I've extended some of my theories a bit, but they're basically only a matter of time," Lest answered. "If what I suspect is true I'll be able to confirm it in about a halfyear more.

"It's a full halfyear since last I saw you here. If certain

stars are in the same position they were in when last you were here I'm probably wrong. If they're where I've predicted then Gaerkt is, indeed, moving around the sun, as are various other of the stars! It's a truly amazing study – despite that I've had so little time to study any of it. *Some* things have happened since last you were here!

"The motions of the stars is quite an absorbing puzzle. It's both complicated and simple at the same time."

"You two have things to discuss that make no sense to me at all!" Marla said. "All that stars and moons stuff is much too complicated to figure out!

"Judge Mako and that awful Captain Gyr just came in. I'll have to speak with Judge Mako about the way those people over near the river are acting. I wish Gyr wouldn't hang around so. I don't entirely trust that man! He inserts himself into conversation in an almost rude manner and at the most importune times!

"Please excuse me, Mikill, but I am deeply concerned with such things. I worry that our little community will deteriorate if we don't keep a constant careful watch on things."

"Yes. Always the community-minded one I'm afraid!" Lest agreed. "I'm sure Mikill will pardon your leaving us. You have no real interest in such subjects."

Z touched his forehead with his index finger in the normal "greetings/ farewell" custom and Marla called out to Mako to wait and left to stand chatting with a small group near the counter.

Z chatted with Lest a few minutes, then went to his room. He would meet Lest at evemeal and the golems would manage to come in at that time. Maita had put the new-style communicators on the shield and had also put back the old-style coms to be detected by Lest. It was safe to communicate quietly in the room now, but may not be wise later. There wasn't yet any reason to watch him.

Your friends at the hill fort are furious and are trying to find some way to retaliate for your death. The golems told them there were men waiting specifically for you to come so it wasn't a matter of simply attacking anyone who came along. They couldn't declare who was behind it, but I made some suggestions through them, asking why Nake and Gyr seemed so opposed to the things you did and why they would send you to the fort to train people when it's supposedly to protect Castiel that you were training them at all. I suggested that you often discussed such things with the golems. I had No suggest he was certain he recognized two of the would-be killers as being with the guard in Castiel, but not the ones that Zho trained. The older officers at the barracks.

"I just hope it doesn't seem too much of a coincidence that I'd show up here as Mikill on the very day Zho was killed," Z said. "I've tried to lay a groundwork for a story if anyone were to question the coincidence."

There can't be any connection, so far as they know.

"Marla and Mako do seem awfully close don't they?" Z asked. "Do you suppose Mako's somehow using Marla to control Lest?"

We'll know that answer when the announcement's made that the result of some kind of spell he used to locate Zho resulted in your untimely death. His reaction to the gory news will show us something about his involvement or lack of same. He's certainly smart enough to be behind it.

"I hate to think he might be," Z replied. "He really is very intelligent and these people need someone like him to discover science for them. He wants knowledge for the single purpose of knowing. He doesn't seek power and I can't accept that's an act. It simply doesn't fit. The more I consider it the less sense it makes."

All we can do now is wait for the golems to deliver their shocking news. We have to know who to move against before we even know what to plan. I think I'm really a lot more interested in preserving King Fonz than I am in worrying about Lest. I've been around him a lot in the golems. He's truly concerned and conscientious.

"We can be pretty sure he's not involved in the worst of it if he's involved at all," Z agreed. "The psychological campaign to turn people against him says he's as much in the dark as we are or more."

Maita caught Z up on what was happening with the others of the crew, then Z rested until time for evemeal.

"The main trouble with that is the water will soon become badly contaminated from the drainage if you divert it upstream," Lest replied to the question a patron asked about getting rid of the wash water from the public pond. "I don't know how to manage it if we don't move the pond downstream from Castiel.

"Ahh! Here's my friend the traveler, Mikill. Perhaps he can solve our problem for us!"

"Certainly! If you tell me what your problem is I guarantee I will suggest a way to solve it, absolutely!" Z replied with a grin.

"That's a foolish statement if'n I ever done heard one!" a woman said. "How you gonna guarantee to solve a problem what you ain't never heard?"

"It's about the disposing of wash water?" Z asked. "I can solve that problem by suggesting no one wash anything anymore. I didn't say the solution was workable – only that I could suggest a way to solve the problem."

"Hah! How would you guarantee to solve the problem where someone has been stealing grain from the city stocks?" Lest asked with a grin. "Surely that isn't so easy to decide!"

"Put everyone who goes within a hundred meters of the place on the island at the mouth of the river and see they're well-guarded so they can never leave!" Z replied, quickly.

"But all'n us goes 'thin a hunnert meters a tha place!" a man argued. "We'd *all* be on tha i-lind!"

"Ah! But there would *not* be any more thefts!" Z replied. "I didn't say you wouldn't have to move the whole population from the city, I only promised I'd stop thefts! That's what a politician does with problems so you've been exposed to that kind of logic before!"

"You'd make a good politician." Lest agreed with a chuckle. "That's exactly the kind of things they propose. Their words are veiled, but that's their meaning."

"Then I sound like a typical politician, not a good one," Z shot back. "What's the real problem?"

Lest told him about the public washing pond and how it was upstream from Castiel, causing the soap and grime to wash right by the town. The land downstream was too rocky to build a pond there.

"Then build the pond to the east," Z suggested. "It's low and marshy back there so all you have to do is build the banks of a pond up, let it fill naturally and let the used water run into the marsh. Marshes are already full of dirt and grime. They're natural filters. We all know that many of those kinds of plants grow well if watered with soapy water so nothing is harmed."

They got into a debate that was settled when they designed a series of three ponds, each a bit lower than the preceding one. The water would collect and settle in the highest and run into the next one where it would be used. The lower one would allow the used water to settle a bit, then the overflow would drain directly into the ten or twelve square kilometer marsh where natural processes would remove any contaminants.

"Well, we've solved that tiny problem!" Gild announced. "The only thing we have to fight is the fact no one will ever do anything about it!"

Marla, Mako and Capt. Gyr had just come into the inn room to listen to the end of the wash argument and to the plan they decided was best.

"I'll see that this is proposed to King Fonz, directly," Marla said. "I'm sure Judge Mako and Captain Gyr will agree to help me present it to him. Maybe we'll be able to convince him to try it!"

"King Fonz is *not* going to expend the labor," Mako said. "I've tried to get this kind of thing to him before. He'll say he'll seek proper advice on it then it dies of neglect."

"Then *I'll* take it to him!" Z suggested. "I'm not from here. Maybe he'll listen to someone who travels and notices the ways things are done elsewhere. When I was here before I got the clear impression the king was very much involved in such projects. Is this the same king, Lest?"

"Er, yes. King Fonz," Lest replied. "I've never known him not to listen to what the people wish of him."

"Well, 'e allus was involved before!" a woman said. "It's jist bin recent here 'e done stopped doin' there things."

"Then I'll prod him into acting," Z promised. "I think anyone who...."

–Shut the nine hells up, Blister Brain!– No snapped, as the golems charged into the room. –I got something to say to all of you! You'd damned well better listen!

–I'm gonna find out who was behind the murder of Zho! I'm gonna make you wish you were never born! I'm gonna make your name known and hated by every damned person in this city! I will also guar-an-blorking-tee you somebody's gonna beg to be allowed to die!–

Lest jumped to his feet, turning over his chair and table.

"Zho?! He's dead?! *Murdered*?!" he cried. "What.... Tell me what happened!"

+Zho was murdered this morning as he rode toward Castiel to speak with Captain Gyr about the games and to King Fonz about a washout on the inner road to the hill fort we found as we were returning to the fort yesterday.

+I have to agree with No about all of this. I will work with him tirelessly until we find who did this thing and I promise we will deal with that person or those persons far more severely than anyone has ever been dealt with in all of history! We *do* have certain powers, you know. We can and *will* find retribution!+

–Severely ain't the word for it, Drone Dome! Kant charged us with taking care of Zho! He's dead! I'm sure gonna make someone very sorry they ever crawled out of the cesspool they called a mother!–

"Who is this 'Zho' person?" Z asked. "What is this about a murder? Tell me what happened."

"Zho was a person who was training the castle guard," Lest answered. "He was very popular with the people and with the guard. I simply can't believe that anyone would want to harm him! I can't accept.... It doesn't make any sense!"

"He wasn't so popular and loved as you may like to pretend," Gyr insisted hotly. "He was insubordinate and he had no sense of security! He flaunted his disdain for authority at every chance!"

–So everyone in town liked him except *you*, hunh?– No said in syrupy tones. –That seems telling, doesn't it? I think that's *very* telling!

–I want to know who anyone is who had any reason to dislike Zho! Yes and I stayed around this city a lot with Zho and the only ones we ever met who didn't like him were *you*, Smug Pug, and Blubber Butt! If we don't have any other suspects – and soon – we'll deal with the lot of you! You can ask Lest here if there's any power known that can stop us!–

"I was right here meeting with Judge Mako all morning!" Gyr cried. "I couldn't have been anywhere near that river road to kill him! I haven't been...." He stopped and looked very scared.

–Who said anything about the river road? *We* most certainly didn't and *we* brought news of Zho's death! That maybe proves you didn't kill him, but you damned well knew where he was killed, so you were involved in *some* way!

–I've *got* your miserable stinking slimy ass good! You're doomed, Blortface! You'd better tell us everything you know – now! It's the only chance you have to stay alive and not begging us to stop!–

"You had someone *killed*?!" Marla cried. "I don't believe it! I always knew you had no morals or ethics, but to ... to, to ... actually commit *murder*?!"

Gyr ran for the door to find the golems blocking the way. He started backing toward the bar.

"It wasn't me! All I did was tell them who to get to do it! I didn't kill anybody!" Gyr whined. "I thought all they would do would be to scare him! Honest! I didn't ... gnnnng!"

Marla screamed. Gyr had backed right into a group of people with Marla and Mako by the bar. Gyr pitched forward with a long heavy carving knife protruding from between his ribs.

+Well! It looks like he won't be telling us who he told or who he told them to get! I wonder if someone in that little group there had reason to want him to stop talking? So *many* things here seem to be rather telling, don't they?

+If you think you're safer now you simply can't think! We

know someone in that group is in this! That's why you killed him – and the *only* reason anyone would have to kill him! You're all seven right there in a tight little wad. Surely one of you saw who stuck him.+

They looked at one another. No one said anything.

–You'll be sorry you ever did that! It shows us that one of you – or more – was in the plot to kill Zho!

–Lest! Can you find who used that knife on him? I ask in the name of Kant!–

Lest went to the knife, shuddered and grasped it. He closed his eyes, gasped, staggered and stood up.

"No. There was far too much emotion. Fear. Terror," he protested. "I can't read anything. It may be mostly from Gyr, not the one who did it.

"I'm sorry."

"I've traveled for many years," Z cried. "I've never seen anything like this! Murders right before my very eyes! What's going on here? What have I walked into? What are those things? What's happening? They're bronze, yet no one seems surprised when they speak!"

"They're golems a sorcerer named Kant made and sent to travel with Zho," Lest explained. "We're used to them.

"I have known of only four or five murders in all my years here in Castiel and those were all because of family fights. I have never before heard of the deliberate murder of another, plotted and planned like the killing of Zho must have been. I have much to think on. I didn't think such things could happen among the people I know and trusted. I don't know how they.... I can't understand any of this! I'm confused!"

"Call the king's guard," Z suggested. "Someone go for the guard. They must be informed about this. Everyone will have to tell them all they know."

"You have seen such things before?" Mako asked.

"Yes. In Flarstrd and Glipkt they have judicial systems that can control crimes of any kind," Z replied. "You were introduced as a judge this afternoon?"

"What does a judge do when there's crime? When part of it happened right before his own eyes?"

"I settle territorial and ownership disputes and serve the king," Mako said stiffly. "I have tried persons for theft, but rarely. I know nothing of these kinds of things!"

"I see. In Glipkt, the judges are in charge of the guard and of direct investigation of all crimes," Z said. "I realize it isn't anything you have experience with, but perhaps you'd better take charge here until authority can be established. The king will surely decide what to do."

They milled about until the guard came, then until King Fonz came running in to be sick at the sight of Gyr, but Fonz quickly directed that Lest and Mako work together. They requested that Z tell them what he knew about the way such things were handled elsewhere.

"They have everyone tell exactly what they saw and heard, then they check to see who was lying," Z answered. "That's about all I know. If someone saw who did it they'll say the wrong thing or do the wrong thing when every-one's story is later compared.

"Did you, er, bronze heads see anything?"

+We're called golems. I'm called Yes and the other is No. We are a creation of Kant, a great wizard.

+I was focused on Gyr. I saw him back into the group there, but didn't see who did it. It was much too fast. I didn't see the knife at all until Gyr fell forward.+

−Yeah. I can say pretty exactly the same thing. I was concentrating on Sludge Bucket, who ended up getting stuck. He was about to tell us who was behind the killing of Zho.−

"Killed Zho?!" King Fonz cried. "What...? Who...? *No!*"

"I was here with Lest," Z said. "I saw Gyr run for the door and the, uh, the golems. Gyr saw they were in front of the door and started backing up saying he didn't kill Zho but he knew who wanted someone else to do it. He said he knew who was behind it and kept backing up until he was among those seven people right there, then he made a sort of grunt and fell. I didn't see the knife or who used it."

"My statement is identical," Lest said. "I tried to read the vibrations from the knife, but there wasn't really anything to tell me...."

The rest of the people said the same thing. Those with Mako and Marla were looking only at the golems and didn't see anything that happened.

+One person saw something!+ Yes suddenly cried. +Marla! You screamed *before* Gyr fell!+

"I, uh, I don't remember why, I was just so, uh...." Marla stammered.

"That's right!" Z replied. "I heard you scream *before* Gyr fell!"

"It was all the blood!" Marla sobbed. "I felt something on my arm and looked down! It was *blood*!"

She staggered and Mako held her up.

"She was right behind him and to his left so she would be the one all the blood spattered on," he pointed out. "There's blood all over that side of her.

"Perhaps if one of you ladies will be kind enough to assist her? Wash the blood off and get her some clean clothes?"

"I'll take 'er home 'n give 'er some strong wine sos she kin mebbe sleep 'er scare off," a woman suggested. "I lives jist past 'er place."

She and another woman took Marla outside, supporting her between them. Marla was saying she wasn't generally nearly so prone to the shaky-scares. The rest of them stayed almost two hours, but nothing new was uncovered. The golems announced they detected sorcery power from Z's medallion and shield and asked about it in Lest's presence. He told them the story he'd told Lest before, then said, "I heard you say you were cast by a sorcerer named Kant.

"Would that be the famous Kant of Dinkard?"

–Yeah, Smog Brain. You heard of him?–

"I don't understand why you call me those awful names," Z protested. "I don't know you! I haven't done anything to you!"

"They call everyone names," Lest soothed. "No does. It means he accepts and likes you if he uses the names in that tone.

"You've heard him speak of Nake. You can certainly hear the large difference in tone."

"Nake? Who's Nake?" Z asked.

–I call him Blubber Butt or Fat Ass or things like that. He's about as much use as tits on a male kirt and weighs about the same as a kirt! Maybe two kirts.–

"I see," Z said. "I've heard of Kant. I understood he was dead. He was very famous and powerful. People liked him.

"I don't see how you could still be working if he made you."

+'Dead' has many meanings. It isn't always like Gyr or Zho. It's sometimes a different thing.+

–Kant's dead like Crapface or Zho, but his life essence has been transferred into a special crystal in a special place. He will awaken every hundred years and take reports from us. We have to report that we let someone kill Zho after we were told to protect him. How would *you* like to tell Kant you failed him? Hunh?–

"Was there any way you could – realistically – have stopped him from being killed if you'd even suspected anyone wanted to kill him?" Z asked. "You seem to desire to blame yourselves for things not in your control."

+We aren't any more logical about emotional issues than you are. We know we aren't guilty of anything, yet we feel a great guilt about Zho's death. It's because we cared so deeply about him. No one here knows the reality of who Zho was or how he was trying to stop ... things, evil things, from happening. We aren't confined by your sense of morality or any other emotional things so we *will* have our revenge and it *will* be terrible beyond your worst comprehension!

+I feel nothing about the murder of Gyr but a rage because he wasn't able to relate who was behind the death of Zho. We will concentrate on that killer now and we *will* find him – or her!

+We will accompany you for a time because you have those power symbols and because you seem able to think when others are confused and stymied.+

"I learned to always do *something* in an emergency long ago," Z said. "If it's the wrong thing someone will say the right thing to do. If it's not wrong it gives the people something to focus on. Once the initial fear and shock, the confusion, have passed most people will do what is necessary."

"You took charge of the situation and made things start, then removed yourself from the responsibility," Lest agreed. "That was almost wise.

"There isn't anything else to do here, but I don't want to go home. I can't offer Marla any comfort and can't cope with any more emotions now. Not hers and not mine."

"I have room," Z offered. "Feel free to stay the rest of the night here."

"No. I believe I'll go to the castle to be with Fonz," Lest replied. "We can discuss this and can ... handle some other things. I'm suddenly much confused about a number of things. I've been used and lied to. I resent that, no matter the direction it came from. I resent being used!"

They parted and Z went to his room. He felt he was being watched so didn't communicate with Maita.

I saw the whole thing through the golems. I saw who stuck Gyr. You should be able to figure that one easily. It could only be one person.

Z was outside the city to collect his thoughts, or so he had reported to Gild when he left at dawn. The golems were floating overhead.

"Marla. That's why she had almost all the blood on her," Z replied. "It seems she's more into this than we'd ever thought possible. Mako's definitely our big brain. I think. I don't know what the deal was with Gyr except that he knew who to get to do various jobs.

"I don't think Lest is involved too deeply. I think that's the thing he resents so much. He realizes his own wife used him in a deadly scheme of some sort.

"It still doesn't quite fit. Marla was coldblooded in the way she killed Gyr. These people don't kill and even King Fonz was physically sick at the sight of death. Most of the people there were shocked and sick, but she didn't show any emotion whatever until she was asked about her scream before Gyr was stuck. She definitely used Lest."

I was watching him through the golems when they charged in with the announcement of Zho's death. He was truly shocked. I think he read that knife and he knows it was Marla who used it and I think he's at the castle to be safe from her. He didn't know she'd go so far.

"He used some spell to know I was leaving the hill fort for Castiel," Z agreed. "He was truly shocked to learn the information was used to commit murder. He knows too much and he's scared. I think you'd better protect him, Maita."

Page 161

I have a floater at a distance. I'll send the golems.

"Good. Maybe he'll confide in the golems," Z suggested. "He respects that they're supposedly the result of a sorcerer's spell. Maybe he'll try to use them to get in touch with the essence or spirit or whatever of Kant.

"Do you think we've prepared the guard well enough to stop whatever kind of takeover ... uh-oh!"

Uh-oh?

"Gyr did come up with hired killers!" Z said. "The golems claimed they had seen the killers among the *old* guard!"

Noted. Six of them. I've used the golems to keep track of them from the first day. They're members of the original military guard thing. They would have been your first students if Nake had trusted you. He gave you the ones you got because he wasn't sure of you or your methods.

"That was what Viz meant when he said not to trust anyone not in the units I trained? It wasn't meant only to not to trust Gyr and Nake?" Z asked.

*Apparently. He warned you to trust *no* one not a mem-ber of the units you trained.*

"I wonder if we can depend on the units I trained to handle those others, then?" Z said. "Do you think you can get something stirred up?"

You get to Lest and Fonz and protect them. I think I have this figured out all the way, now! The golems are going to the hill fort and they're bringing back your unit and Kad. We can finish this project now. I'm not being misdirected and I'm not being manipulated and I'm not accepting any impossible excuses for one damned thing!

Z felt the excitement in Maita's tones and grinned. It was time for a little action!

"It's the only way any of it makes any sense," Z insisted to Fonz and Lest. "There was a drop of blood here and there on two other people, but Marla had it all over one arm and down the side. She was pressed against him as he was stabbed and the knife had to go right into his heart. The blood gushed and only the person who stabbed him would find it impossible to avoid getting it all over herself. I think you read that knife, Lest. I think it told you very surely Marla was the one who used it. I think you're here right now because she knows you read it and she has no compunction against killing you or anyone else who gets in her way. She's not sane. You have to know that. I know you want to protect her and ask for an explanation you know she can't give, but the facts are right there. Refusing to see them won't help anyone. It could even kill more people, you included.

"Did she trick you into telling her when that fellow who was murdered would be where he could be killed?"

Lest released a shuddering sigh and nodded.

"I don't know what this is about," Fonz said. "Why would she kill anyone? What could she hope to gain?"

"She's building a large army to attack your neighboring communities to set herself up as some kind of queen," Z replied. "That would be my guess."

"But, but *why*?!" Fonz exploded. "*Why* would anyone want this responsibility? I would very *gladly* let her be queen of Castiel if she could fill the office! I would *welcome* a chance to get away from this awful King of Castiel necessity! I'm king only in that I have an inherited responsibility and so have received the special education necessary to be able to cope with all these problems that keep coming up that makes me stay.

"Lest, you're my friend. You know I want to be able to study the world and the stars. We spend what little time I have of my own talking about those things. I don't understand why anyone would *want* this kind of thing hanging over his life! I can't even choose my own mate! It was only the most fantastic good fortune that Gola is so perfectly matched to me! Do you know how many times in history a wife of a king of Castiel has died of some sickness she didn't have? How many of its kings have done the same? How could she hope to ever accomplish any such thing alone, anyway? It doesn't make any sense!"

"I imagine she has a first officer in Mako and had a second officer in Gyr," Z replied. "Maybe Gyr and Nake both are second officers. It's those two who came up with the idea to.... Get Viz in here! He knows something and she'll have him killed if she finds it out!"

Fonz sent a message to Viz to report for special king's duty assignment and he was in the room a few minutes later. Z asked him what he knew and said they knew all about Marla and Mako and the old guard unit, who were committing murder at Gyr's orders.

"I don't know anything about Marla," Viz replied. "I do know Mako and Nake are planning to oust King Fonz and take over the city for themselves. I never trusted those old officers. You all have to know none of us trusted them. We made that plain enough! They don't care about people, somehow, if you see what I mean. They're very cold and very hard.

"Is it true they killed Zho?"

Z was suddenly worried. There wasn't any way he could know about Viz – at all – and he'd just blabbed out that Viz was in danger because of what he knew! That could be a very bad move! He had to keep in mind at all times that he wasn't supposed to have information from Zho!

"How did you know Viz knew anything?" Lest asked with a strange look in his eye – just what Z had feared!

–Because I *told* him, Swamp Breath!– No snarled as the golems came floating into the room. –We have Dense Dome and Zho's unit coming as fast as they can. They should be here in about three and a half hours. They're going to push their kirts to the full limits of endurance, but those kirts have been in training so they'll make it. We're going to have our revenge on this bunch! There's no way anyone's gonna get away with killing Zho! No way! I intend to see every one of the rocktoads who were any part of that suffer like they won't believe!–

+It is good that someone not involved in this in any way was here for us to confide in and we thank you, Mikill. Your logic was perfect it seems. We couldn't see very much of it because we were much too emotionally involved. We were not only charged with the protection of Zho, he was our friend and confidant.

+We will have to strike in a concerted move. Viz, Tor, Wil and Yan can give you the information. Kad, Sto, Eil, Jok and Tig can act in the manner they were trained to act. I believe they all will respond properly to commands when they understand there is no other way. They very much liked and respected Zho and can see the remaining danger all of the people of Castiel, indeed, all the people of Gaerkt itself are under the cloud of with this distressing and....+

–AHHHHHH! SHUT THE HELLS UP, BLATHER BRAIN!– No screamed. (Z jumped and bumped into Lest, who almost grinned.) –Do you *have* to be such a flaptongued idiot? *Why* can't you simply say a thing and let it go?–

"Don't start that crap now," King Fonz warned soberly. "We must find a way to neutralize the people who are in this. There must *not* be another killing. I don't know how to deal with this!"

"I understand this Zho person trained a guard unit specially in some fort as well as one here," Z said. "If he was anything like what the golems described to me they

Page 165

were trained specifically for this one thing. I think probably Zho was a *very* perceptive person. I think, being from Dinkard he knew a lot about these kinds of things. The life there is very different in some ways from life here. It is not so easy."

–He knew this would happen, Pouch Puss! We've seen it two or three times before. He even *told* us some people were gonna get a surprise some day when his troops did exactly what they were being trained to do!

–Yes and I know what he knew. We know what's to come. We know Zho, as much as he hated the thought, knew what would have to be done and how damned hard it would be for decent people.

–You kirt paddy idiots are going to learn something about the evil side of the nature of people!–

+Now, No! Be nice! I'm sure Mikill clearly understands what Zho was doing. *He* is also a very perceptive type of person.

+I remember the time in Horstadtkium when those bandits were frightening the settlers near Green Forest and how Zho trained the men there to do ex*act*ly the right thing! He was....+

–YEEEESH! HERE WE GO AGAIN! Dense Dome is on another of his ten hour reminiscence binges!–

"You believe Zho trained the troops for this specific thing?" King Fonz asked. "I don't begin to understand what you mean. He trained them to fight ... of course! He trained them to fight trained troops – which is what they will have to fight here! The guards Mako, Gyr and Nake trained before he even came here are the ones who must be defeated! How very true! How amazingly foresighted!"

"We had several discussions where he even told me the troops were being trained to fight other troops – and there were no troops anywhere but here!" Lest cried. "He *told* me what he was planning! I just didn't see it!

"Well, I think I have a problem I must solve myself. My mate is, as you've noted, not entirely sane. I've seen signs of that at times. She was far too interested in what Zho was teaching the guards. I don't know how to proceed."

"You have to wait until the guard's defeated, then we have to take care of the dual problem of Nake and Mako," Fonz suggested. "Perhaps a way will become clear. Don't go to her now, my old friend. She'll kill you without thought."

+We'll all have to wait until the units prove Zho was right. If he miscalculated there the rest is irrelevant.+

"First let me say that I was asked to handle this by those golems," Z began. "I don't really know much about what happened here except for the things they, Viz, Lest, Fonz and certain others have told me. When you see my information is incorrect or incomplete it is vital that you tell me. That is the only way we can even hope to be successful here.

"I'm to tell you what has to be done, but the golems want to tell you something your dead friend Zho wanted told."

Kad, Sto, Eil, Jok and Tig had ridden into Castiel only a few minutes before. The golems had met them on the road and led them directly to the castle where Lest, Fonz, Z, Yan, Tor, Viz and Wil were waiting. Z had refrained from saying too much until they were all assembled together, but the golems, Lest and Fonz had "explained" the whole situation to him in front of the unit from Castiel.

–Open your ears and listen! This is the time for what Zho taught you to be put into use. This is the reason he taught you. You all know by now that Zho was murdered on the road by the river. Yes and I saw the whole thing. We flew to the fort to tell those of you from there, then we came back here where we met Flap Yap and made a plan.–

+You could hold back with the cutesies until this is over,+ Yes said haughtily. +What No says is true. We saw the people who murdered Zho. We came here because we didn't know what else to do and because we knew the murder plot had to come from this city.

+Mikill has a good mind and carries certain power symbols and amulets given to him by a sorcerer. We know with certainty he can be trusted because of those things. A sorcerer does *not* give such items to anyone who is deceitful or devious.+

–What Doodle Mouth is trying to explain is that we can trust Mikill. He said for us to try to find the people who were out there by the river road and who killed our friend.

–We did! They're the old guard who were trained by Gyr and Nake before Zho came here.

–We swore revenge for Zho's death and we mean to have it! Mikill, Lest and King Fonzie found who's behind the whole thing. Mikill made a plan after we told him what we knew about how Zho trained you so we'll let him tell you what you have to do now. We won't be able to consider the subject objectively. We're so upset and mad we'd screw it up to where too many innocent people would be hurt or even killed. I don't need that on my head!–

"We have found that Nake and Judge Mako controlled most of this thing from the first, but that they were, in turn, controlled by Lest's own wife, Marla," Z said. "Lest knew nothing about it until he connected the fact Marla tricked him into finding where Zho would be at a certain time. That information resulted in Zho's death.

"Zho was a very close friend to Lest from his first day in Castiel when they had conversations about things the sorcerer who made the golems was studying. Lest could no longer accept the excuses Marla and others gave for what was happening and was shocked and horrified that anyone, much less his own wife, would do such things. Such things are not any part of the people here.

"Marla isn't quite sane, but she's very cunning and very dangerous.

"I think some of you will know the old guard. I think you know some of them are totally without normal Gaerkt capacities for compassion. I think you know they're dangerous to all that we hold to be decent.

"The plan was to displace King Fonz, take over the city,

train the men in the guard to kill and to establish some kind of large political entity where Marla would be queen and Nake and Mako would be her priests or whatever they call those people."

"What about Gyr?" Sto asked. "I knew that one! He's in this up to his ugly ears!"

"Marla killed him because she was afraid he'd tell us about the plot," Fonz answered. "Yes and No backed him into a cave and the only way out was to tell them who was head of the scheme that led to Zho's death. She stabbed him through the heart."

–We'll personally take care of Rock Head and Pebble Brain and her. Mikill knows what Zho was training you for because we saw this sort of thing before and he knew exactly where *that* stream entered the river!–

"You were trained to fight a trained force – while there *are* no other trained forces," Z explained. "Zho knew the time soon would come when the old guard would have to be challenged. Perhaps he felt he wouldn't be alive to fight that final battle himself, but you are ready. You are his legacy to right and decency.

"From what King Fonz tells me there are twenty four of the old guard who were trained in these kinds of things. They were trained by Nake and Gyr.

"Zho knew very much what kinds of things they were trained for, thus he concentrated on those skills that would make you most useful in resisting what they know.

"King Fonz, Lest, the golems and I will handle Nake, Marla and Mako. You will have to make a simultaneous attack on the old guard."

+We have found the old guard are at their barracks and are preparing to fight you from in there. They are now establishing themselves where they can use the crossbows Nake so loves to try to hold you away from their position.

You have been taught by Zho what he calls the 'range' of those weapons and how to avoid them from any position. You will be in the gravest of dangers should you approach near to those facilities so we have a plan suggested by Mikill to thwart those poorly-conceived strategies.+

–Wobble Jaw means we've seen the obvious weakness of such a stupid plan. They depend on the fact no one else here is trained to kill anyone – but they don't realize *you* are!–

"What Nul Noggin means is that Zho *did* train you to kill!" King Fonz said, getting grins from several of the guard at his comeback to No's depictions of others. "He only did it in such a way that you would respond to your better inner natures and wouldn't ever do it for personal motives."

–Salt Brain means you damned well *will* kill such as those guards because they killed Zho! You won't kill for yourselves, but you'll damned well kill to protect the innocent people in Castiel and to revenge the murder of Zho!–

"If they're barricaded in the barracks – Hey! I finally see where the terms connect – how will we get them out?" Kad asked.

"Simple," Z replied. "They have no food and we can take the water trough out. Then we will sit back past crossbow range and wait."

–They'll figure what you're doing as soon as I announce it. They'll come out of there with their crossbows and you'll have to decoy them. You have to make them fire their crossbows at you while you're out of range.

–They don't really have the right training for that kind of thing, but you gotta be careful or they'll get you one at the time. There're a lot more of them than of *you*! Don't forget that fact or there'll soon be even more of them than you because a few of you will be dead!–

"*But*! It takes way too long to reset a crossbow!" Viz cried.

"That's the first thing Zho taught us. We make them fire, then ride in and get them before they refit."

"They're trained to fire in a sequence," Fonz warned. "You have to find a way to make them break that training. You have to make them believe they will have time to refit if they fire too soon."

"Perhaps the power held in this shield will be useful there!" Z said triumphantly. "All it can do is blind an enemy for a few seconds, but that should be enough!

"Kad, you're more used to command. You're a captain so I want you to deploy these men evenly around the barracks to be sure no one leaves. Stay out of crossbow range. I'll repeat that as many times as I have to. I want no one to doubt the foolishness and danger if you forget that because it's all they have. You can't allow it to work in *their* favor!"

Kad nodded sharply and led the men out of the chamber.

–Whadda you mean the shield can blind an enemy?– Z knew that was from Maita.

"It stores light and can release it in a blinding flash," Z answered. "That leaves the enemy blind for long enough to stick a sword through his heart. Figure on two to three seconds. No more. It will leave the old guard blind for long enough if they start and are moving when the flash is released. Zho's units can ride in fast – if what I've been told is true – and they won't be able to see them to use the crossbows on them. They will be coming from a direct angle when the flash is released, then will move about two meters to the left as it flashes and the bowmen who have drawn the target will fire where the kirtsmen *were*, not where they *are*.

"Shall we go to Judge Mako's chambers first or Nake's?"

"What will we do with them?" Fonz asked.

"Confine them in the castle criminal detention cells," Lest suggested. "They are generally empty and are secure. We can figure on something to keep them from harming anyone else later."

They marched to the judge's chambers and barged in with Z in front. He had the "shield" held in a defensive position. Mako was behind his desk and Nake was on a wide low divan. They were both jerking and gasping in some kind of violent contortions. Someone was running out of the rear doorway so the golems raced to get ahead of that one.

"It's a strong poison in the wine," Lest said, touching the decanter on the desk. "Someone – we can deduce who – poisoned the wine and fed it to them only a very few moments ago. I think there is no saving them. I can't say I'm sorry."

Luxe ran into the room pursued by the golems.

"Luxe?!" King Fonz demanded.

"You poisoned your own father?!" Lest cried.

"I came in and *found* them like that!" Luxe screamed.

Nake rolled off the divan and gurgled, pointing at her.

–I think not, Bounce Butt! Rearus Ponderosus there accuses you positively and directly! We have identification by a dying man.–

Nake jerked once more and was dead.

"Where is Marla?" Lest asked.

"At her house!" Luxe cried. "She said it was just a potion you made that would make them forget everything that happened for seven years! I swear! She said it was only a potion!"

"Too bad you didn't taste it to be sure," Z said. "I don't believe for a single second you didn't know exactly what it was.

"Shall we call on Marla?"

"Guard! Judge's Guard!" Fonz yelled. Two guards came in from the front of the building and Fonz told them to take Luxe to the criminal holding cell and see she didn't get out.

"Well, we had best bring Marla here I imagine," Lest said. "I admit to not feeling ... much of anything about her."

Marla was gone. She had taken a few things and ridden out of town in a carriage a few minutes before, headed along the river road downriver.

"She's from the islands," Lest suggested. "She'll be able to hide there. We won't be able to catch her. Maybe we'd better do what we can about that guard she left as her legacy to Castiel.

"She knows island people – but I think they won't have her!"

"Well, the guard're completely surrounded and we've stopped the water," Kad reported. "They have their one barrel, but it won't last long for twenty four of them. They shot a few bolts at us, but we were too far away for them to have any effect and they've threatened to kill us all if we don't retreat. They say they can use the crossbows at more of a distance than we can use our standard bows so I told them we have some crossbows, too. It's sort of like a starebird-gronserpent affair. We're all reasonably safe so long as we stay as we are, but anything could change the situation and the outcome isn't sure either way."

"I think Mikill has the answer for that!" Fonz said. "He's going to use the golems?"

"Yeah," Z replied. "I'll use both the golems and the magic shield. I think part of them will come out the en-trance here, part will stay inside and some might try to get out the other side of the compound. The only question I have is whether most will come out this way or the other."

+I think perhaps we might have the same powers built into our base plate as you have in the shield. You can stay here with Kad and this unit and we'll go around back with Viz and the other unit. We can choose the right moment to blind them. I think we should probably try to impress upon our fellow soldiers that we will have a very limited time to act once we use the flashing spell so it would perhaps be best the men be mounted on their kirts and prepared to act instantly. As Zho instructed earlier they should be moving when the spell is released and should move to the side if any have drawn target. It will prove most advantageous if all are prepared to act....+

–Sheeee! Get their lazy asses on the kirts and tell them to be ready to charge as soon as the light flashes! There ain't no probably or perhaps about it, Lint Brain! They're gonna have to move fast!–

"What we'll do is have the golems incite them," Z said. "If we can make them charge before they have time to think we can more easily defeat them. Ride like you were at that festival thing Lest and the golems have told me about. Do the jumps and the hurdles and the zag-track runs. The only difference is that the targets are the old guard instead of a bunch of sand in a bag.

"They killed Zho. They'll also kill you if you hesitate. Tell the men to picture themselves as riding the practice course. Picture that bunch as being the targets and *don't* think of them as anything else!

"This is against our nature, but it *must* be done! If we fail here many innocent people will die at their hands."

+I guess there isn't anything else to do but to go in there and see what we can stir up in that caldron. I think we should have some plan as to how to make sure they act immediately. If they hesitate and don't come out in a single group we're at a great disadvantage due strictly to the difference in numbers. You must be prepared to take into consideration that the enemy is....+

–Not *now*, you idiot! This is the worst possible time for one of your filibusters! *I'll* get them out of there!–

The floater started moving toward the barracks. Z waved

for the units to get into place.

–Awright in the barracks! You can come out here with your hands on top of your heads and not carrying anything or we're gonna set that whole damned place on fire! We're magic golems and we damned well *can* do just that so don't think we're gonna be soft around your type! I'd personally like to see every one of you slimy slugseekers burn! Slowly! Starting at the feet and moving up at maybe a centimeter per hour!

–You got one minute, dud heads!–

They flew quickly over the building and toward the rear gate to the compound. Z grinned and waved for the troops to get their mounts ready.

Nothing happened for a minute, then the golems scooped up some rocks onto their floater, went above the buildings, dropped them, then went quickly back to wait with the second unit.

"Those little rocks won't do anything to them!" Fonz protested.

"You know that and I know that – but the ones inside do *not* know that!" Z said. "The golems said they'd fire the building, the ones inside can see nothing, the minute's up and there are noises on the roof. What would you do?"

"I can add a bit to the effect," Lest said. He took some powder from a pouch, mixed it carefully and waved at the golems to come over. He gave them the powder and said to drop it on the roof and to add a drop of water. The golems floated over the building and soon billows of greywhite smoke began pouring from the roof and drifting slowly downward.

"It only makes a lot of smoke that goes down instead of up," Lest explained. "As you've noted, *they* won't know that!"

–Hey! Arrow Bait!– No yelled from the rear. –There

seems to be a bit of a fire on your roof! You think maybe your one little barrel of water might put it out?–

The door to the barracks flew open and eight men with drawn crossbows came running out. Z held up a hand, waited until they were a few meters short of range for the crossbows, dropped his hand and had the shield release an intense white directed laser beam at them, blinding them momentarily.

Kad yelled, "Charge!" and they were off.

It was over very quickly and Z breathed a sigh of relief that the unit had actually shot the old guard. He hadn't been at all sure they would, but they were truly incensed about Zho. They had reacted perfectly. Kad took a bolt in his left thigh and Yan was killed in the attack on the rear. Z had hoped there wouldn't be any casualties among the units, but that was gone.

Sixteen of the old guards were killed, leaving only eight inside the building. Z had seven trained troops to use against them, but could wait. Lest attended to Kad while the others held a short ceremony in honor of Yan. It was spontaneous and was deeply touching. It also solidified the repugnance of the men against the rest of those guards inside and Z had to restrain them from rushing in.

"You can't hope to fight them so long as they're in there!" he warned. "You can't ride your kirts into a hail of crossbow bolts while they can shoot from the slits and windows and you can't even see them."

Yan's body was soon taken away and the units waited for Z's further orders.

Z went to Kad, who said it was a flesh wound, painful, but not too terribly serious since Lest had removed the bolt and had stopped the worst bleeding. Z took some bacitracin ointment from the shield synthesizer, said it was a salve given to him by the sorcerer who made the shield and also gave him a good dose of tetracycline in juice to prevent any serious infection, saying the juice contained a potion to stop pain.

"We'll have to figure some way to get those others out of there," Z said. "We can't fight them from here and I don't want to have to wait six or eight days for them to be starved out."

+There has been quite enough violence. I am thoroughly sickened by this scourge I know it's unavoidable, but I am not designed for this kind of thing! If we can simply stand guard at all times here until they are out of food and water they will come out. I think we must plan carefully how we will handle the situation at that time. We must find a way to avoid becoming anything like....+

–IDIOT! We got to get them. Period! They are *killers*, in case it escaped your attention!–

"We can put them in the criminal cell where Luxe is," Fonz said. "We can find a method to ensure they are of no more danger to the people here."

"They'd still be a danger to people wherever they went," Z warned. "We have to find a way to keep them around, but to keep the people safe from them."

–Look, Clutter Brain! There ain't no way we can let them run around here and there ain't no way we can turn them loose on other people either! You got something to face that there ain't no way around! You hate it, I hate it, the rest of us hate it, but it's still there and it's not going away!–

"Where is Lest?" Fonz asked suddenly. "He should be able to do something with all that sorcery he studies!"

Z looked around then, but couldn't locate the sorcerer anywhere. The golems spun and started back toward the barracks just as black smoke began curling up from the rear of the building. Lest soon came out from behind the building, crawling under the shooting slots and windows.

He moved to the front corner and sat where he could see the door.

Z waved for the units to mount their kirts, then they waited for something more to happen.

When the entire rear wall of the building was on fire the door burst open and the guards came out shooting their deadly crossbows wildly in all directions. The units waited until they were reloading to charge. It was over very quickly. Two kirts were shot and Viz took a bolt in his lower left arm, but it wasn't too terribly serious. The bacitracin salve and tetracycline would ensure he didn't get any infection from it.

"That would seem to handle all of this except for my wife," Lest said as he finished wrapping the wound. "I seriously doubt we'll ever hear from her again unless she finds another place to start the same kind of thing. Without a sorcerer for a husband and connections with the local king I doubt she could be successful.

"We can hope it is over for all time. I want to be able to study the motions of the stars and the way plants grow and do many things and to never again have to deal with anything even remotely like this!"

"It's the ideas she was able to infect such others as Nake, Gyr, Mako and Luxe with that are dangerous, not her," Fonz said. "I worry she will be able to catch the ear and eye of another."

"She works on the baser traits of anyone," Z suggested. "She's very deliberate about it and works to a definite plan – which is why everyone thought her to be a pillar of the community while she worked her scheme right in front of them. I worry she might find another place like Castiel.

"You say she was from the islands?"

"Yes. The cluster. There are many hundreds of them and they can't all be searched," Lest answered.

"I know a little about them," Z replied. "I spent some time there so I can possibly find her.

"I think that's important. I think I have to go out there to warn people about her if nothing more."

"That is a large project," Fonz said.

"It's most fortunate I have no other work then, isn't it?" Z replied. "Perhaps I've at last found a purpose to my life and to my wanderings!"

"Perhaps the sorcerer who made that shield had a far greater influence on you than you know," Lest agreed. "I plan to keep a close watch on things here for so long as I live. If I find an unanswerable question such as that about training guards in violence I will demand I *do* find an answer!"

"I think we will all be far more concerned with such things," Fonz agreed. "I have another great problem. I have a guard who are trained in precisely those things!"

+Those guards were needed at one time and for one specific purpose. You must impress upon them that there is no shame in anything they have done here. They acted as they did in great sacrifice for the aid of all the people. They must be made to understand that they have done no wrong! Circumstances dictate what is right at a given time. Their sacrifice was tremendous. Greater than that of any of the rest of us. They had to act completely contrary to the nature of all good men. They had to put civilization aside for those they know and love and for a short time or the people controlling those guards would have put it aside for all for many years.

+Perhaps there is a deep philosophical point here. I can understand that to act in such a manner in normal circumstances carries a burden of shame no one could bear. Perhaps the very minds of the old guard were beyond redemption *because* they were made to act in that very manner when they killed Zho. I think the very essence of decency was drained from them by this plot as was that of Nake and Gyr and Mako and Luxe. I think Marla was probably born deficient. I think probably she never *had* any such normal tendencies and that she wouldn't be capable of ever understanding that *she* was the one who was different.

+I suggest with the wisdom of Kant directly that the units should be honored for their great and terrible sacrifice, not held in disdain for the things that terrible sacrifice made necessary. Circumstances often alter circumstances. This was not a normal time and it was not a normal situation. It was not a normal demand.

+I extend the deepest gratitude to the units. I will always deeply honor them for their heroism here. I am, for once in my existence, sure that No agrees with me.

+We will go with Mikill to seek Marla. We also have to act in a manner contrary to our very nature – because our nature is that of he who made us and he was a good and decent man.+

–I have to agree fully with Butter Brain. There is no shame in anything any of the survivors here have done. It was needed for the protection of all and for their children and grandchildren.–

Z didn't say anything, but he wondered very much what that was all about.

"Thank you," Kad said. "I was worried about what we did, but I realize we had no choice. If we *didn't* do that everyone would suffer. We did it because of our anger and also from something that told us it must be done. I think Zho left us with the sure knowledge we would someday have to stand to evil. I think we did that. I have no shame!"

"True. As Yes said, circumstances must dictate reality," Fonz agreed. "The reality was that we must act in a manner to stop a greater evil. We did that. There is no shame.

"I thank each of you for your great sacrifice in the name of the people of Castiel and of Gaerkt. By authority of the king you are hereby now and forever absolved of any responsibility for anything done today. Honor dictated actions. Circumstances dictated only one right course and you followed that course with determination."

"There are things that must be done and times they must be done," Z said. "We were here at this time and place, thus were morally bound to act in the only honorable manner we *could* act and still consider ourselves decent people. It's as simple as that."

The speeches were over. He'd left himself a way to get far from Castiel and to have the golems go with him, but he still wasn't sure what the speeches were about. They didn't seem the kind of thing Maita would do or that the golems' computer would come up with.

In the morning he suggested he'd have to get after Marla as quickly as possible if there was to be any hope of finding her. He left for the islands from the point at the river mouth in the early afternoon. Wil and Sto had accompanied him to the docks so he never had a chance to speak with Maita until the following day on the first of the islands he stopped at. Maita would send floaters to locate Marla, wherever she was. He could be sure of that!

"Awright! First question is what the hell all the speeches were about back there?" Z demanded when he was at last alone. "I know very damned well it wasn't your idea!"

Heleemius and Zianteus were here with me. I watched what was happening and called them. Heleemius said to do that.

"What was the point?" Z asked. "I trained them for exactly that kind of thing!"

*If they were honored for being militaristic and violent it

would start the very thing in this race we came here to stop. The M Eighty Seconds know how those things work and injected the psychological direction that such things might be necessary, but there was tremendous shame to those same actions when they were *not* of the imperative! Your training was slanted more toward making games out of the military arts while preparing them to defend.*

+We strongly impressed them with the feeling that it was *excusable* to act like that in defense of *others*, but it was never acceptable to even think of doing such things aggressively. We hoped to leave the thought that these things aren't ever right to contemplate. If this is needed it is a product of the circumstances at the time and is to be thought of only in that context.+

"I know what you're trying to say," Z replied. "You have to reach a balance that wouldn't give anyone any glory for *what* he did, but only for *why* he did it."

*Close enough. No brave soldiers here. This culture definitely does *not* need anything like that. We can't glorify the military mind in any form.*

"What will they do with Luxe?" Z asked.

They'll have to work that out for themselves. That much of a moral dilemma is good for them and can be a teaching tool to Fonz, who I happen to like a lot. I finally like Lest a lot. You did all along.

–Monster Boobs is our problem now. We've got our own kind of moral dilemma with her. What do we do? Z was right when he said she doesn't know she's any different from anyone else. She thinks everyone hides her greeds and they're all playing some stupid game.–

You're probably right. I've got twenty floaters out looking for her so it shouldn't take long. Her boobs aren't very much out of proportion. You shouldn't use Z's expressions in places like this where they aren't common terms.

–We're the only ones here, Gasket Girdle! I sure ain't that stupid! HE'S the one who prattles on about things he shouldn't know anything about. It's a good thing none of them had the time to wonder how he knew so much about what Zho taught the units and how he even knew everyone's names in those units when he'd never met any of them before!–

+You did tend to speak knowledgeably about a large number of subjects you shouldn't have known about, Z. If Lest or Fonz ever thinks about it after the emotional stress period has passed they'll be stricken immediately with the fact you seemed to have far more information about far too many people and things to consider as logical or even possible. I couldn't think of a way to warn you at the time that you had a great amount of data at your disposal that Mikill simply could *not* have....+

–AHHHHH, SHUT UP, TUNNEL HEAD! Just say he should learn when to stop blubbering on and on and on! I think he must have learned that blabberiness from *you*!–

Blabberiness?

"It seems we can relax a bit now," Z sighed. "It's good to know things are almost back to normal – I think."

–We got to search all over this pile of rocks out here in this swamp they call a world! Maybe that *is* normal!–

+Now, No! Don't be so negative! *You* don't have to search anything at all!

+I think these islands are like perfect green jewels set in a delightful blue sea! The fragrance of the myriad cascades of flowers wafting in on the cool breezes always makes us....+

–*What*?! ARE YOU COMPLETELY MAD?! We're bronze! We can't *smell* anything! What the hell is all this crap about cool breezes? We can stand up to several hundred degrees Maitan or down to near absolute zero! What did I ever do to deserve this curse?–

They floated away, Yes saying, +Now, No. I have a highly developed sense of beauty and can *imagine* how the fragrances of cascades of flowers so nicely described by the poets would make the....+

–AAAARRRRRGGGGHHHHH!–

She was on Lorgletelt Island to your direct south early this morning, but sailed away on the tide. There are some dozens of islands that can be reached in only a few hours and there are many more dozens of boats out there. I have to be careful about approaching too close with the spy floaters, but I think I know which boat she's on. It's got a large closed cabin so she can stay inside and I can't totally be sure. I need a suggestion or two!

"Where are the golems?" Z asked. "Isn't she supposed to be the primary person they want revenge on? Didn't they vow to find anyone connected with Zho's death?"

Good idea! I can send them out to check any boat I want with a built-in reason! You seem to be awfully taken with that island. What gives?

"I've found a bunch of varieties of what look a lot like Restrepias and Masdevalias growing in the mosses on some tree trunks," Z answered. "I figured I might as well collect a few orchids while I'm here."

I usually try to locate them for you when we're on a world. I didn't find too much here other than those things and what appears to be a Dracula. There's something on the southern end of the continent to your west that looks like a red Sophronitis. They're all over the place.

Z collected orchid-like plants on any world he was visiting so would take specimens back to EC of all the types he found on Gaerkt to add to his collection. He had the largest and finest assortment of such plants in the galaxy on his personal island there. Artists from Parf and New Zule traveled across the galaxy (No big deal in the Maitan

Empire with the TTH4 drive) to paint them.

Z went out to look around while Maita directed the golems. It wasn't long before Maita reported that Marla hadn't been on that particular boat. There would have to be a systematic search conducted.

"I'm finally enjoying this place," Z said. "We aren't in any hurry so simply follow all the boats she *could* be on and see which one she gets off of." He found what looked like a weird cross between a Phaius and a Gongora a bit later and collected a specimen.

She wasn't on any of the boats that could have been around there at the time. That means she got off of one of them between the time she left and I started watching all of them. That means she has to be on one of four islands. I can scan all of them. Only one is big enough to take much time, Missenfrckt.

Two hours later, *She has to be on Missenfrckt. Get in your little boat and come on. I'll send a tug floater to pick up your orchids and drag you to fairly close, then you can sail on in normally. The golems can come with you and you can tell her the magic shield made noises when it was moving in her direction or something equally stupid. I think Lest tried to locate her with some kind of spell, but she knows about that one and can thwart it.*

Z sighed and got into the fast little boat Maita made from a local design to be pulled a few kilometers out from Missenfrckt. He sailed in on the breeze and tied the boat to the anchoring post. The golems floated a few feet overhead as he strolled casually toward the local inn. People would stop to stare at them, so Yes greeted everyone while No made snide remarks. Several got into the spirit of it and started trading replies with No – to be solidly and quickly defeated. It was great fun and lent a festive air to the walk.

Z took a room and went to the pub for beer and a stew. He

wanted Marla to know they were there and that she'd either have to confront them or try to hide. Maita had a small patch on the base of the golems' floater that showed Z exactly where she was in relation to him at all times. She seemed to be staying in one place.

More and more people came to see the magic golems and to try to best No in vulgar acidic insults. Yes pretended terrible embarrassment at the way No was acting in a place where they were guests.

When Marla started moving Z was at the center of a large group and couldn't follow her. Maita would keep her under close scrutiny so she couldn't move anywhere he couldn't locate her easily.

Z didn't know how he could handle any confrontation with a lot of people around. He didn't have any reason to care if she lived or died, but wanted to be absolutely certain there wasn't anyone else involved with it. That would mean getting her away somewhere and using the probe. Since she was definitely behind the supposed death of Zho and directly killed Nake and Mako there was no prohibition even under Maita's strict rules to using the probe on her. She in effect stood convicted of a capital crime.

She only moved a short distance away and was again stationary, so Z assumed she'd simply moved to another house or inn somewhere east of him a little more than three kilometers. She was at about eight hundred meters elevation. That was all the information the golem's readout gave him so he could deduce she was staying on the coastal cliffs in some castle up there. There were several. That also meant she knew some very important people on this island. That probably meant she intended to start the whole sordid thing over out here.

He'd go calling in the morning. She wasn't likely to move again and Maita would watch her if she did, so he settled back and enjoyed the evening. He even met a nice girl who was as taken with him as he was with her. Gaerkt society was open sexually to unmarried people, so he enjoyed a pleasant night, indeed!

She's in the castle right about here. It's really quite an impressive edifice, if I may sound like Yes for a short moment. The place seems to be virtually deserted, but those castles here are usually occupied by a single family and they don't have servants in any real sense.

Z had the screen folded out from his shield and watched the clear projection Maita sent. It was of a castle that he'd seen in the earlier scenes Maita had shown him to familiarize him with the islands. It really was impressive.

"Is it some kind of king or something such?" Z asked. "Do you have any way to know anything about the owner?"

A sorcerer. Probably an old friend of Lest. I couldn't get the floater close enough to hear anything, but there are some small psy readings There are the regular trapping of someone who is studying sciences on a primitive level.

Z sighed, went downstairs to the pub for some cav and warm sweetcakes, then went out with the golems overhead to stroll up the coast road. People would greet him and the golems, but No refused to be baited into another insult session and they were soon alone on the road.

The weather was nice for hiking, but a storm was gathering that would strike before he reached the castle. He mumbled about how fitting that seemed.

The rain started when he was a few hundred meters from the castle, as did a lot of lightning. He dodged into the high arch at the entrance where there was a big sign welcoming visitors. It said to go in, so he did. That sign was like the one he'd noted at Fonz's castle in Castiel and seemed to be the custom here.

He found himself in a large arched room with massive doors at various spots and a stairway curving up to a second floor. There was a low railing around the circular second story behind which were several more doors.

+She's in the room behind the second door from the top of the stairs,+ Yes reported quietly, so Z trotted up the stairs to pull the bell cord by that door. It opened after a minute and Marla saw Z and the golems, gasped and tried to slam the heavy door. The golems were too quick and dodged inside, then Z pushed in immediately behind them and closed the door.

+We promised we'd find you and take our revenge on you!+ Yes announced, so Z knew there was some kind of listening device in the room.

"I don't know what you're talking about!" she cried. "I came here for some relaxation! What are you talking about!?"

That showed Z that she knew there was a listener. It was probably the sorcerer who owned the place. It was certainly logical that a sorcerer would know they were in his castle so she would try to convince him that Z was the bad guy while she was innocent of anything.

"Lest would surely have contacted your host here if your visit were proper," Z replied. "I'm sure he didn't. I'm sure you've blocked his ability to communicate with your host.

"Luxe was caught when she gave your little potion to Nake and Judge Mako. There's some slight chance she really didn't know the stuff was designed to kill them. She might really have believed it was merely a forgetfulness potion – but I doubt it greatly.

"There are twenty nine people who are dead because of your plots. Zho was the real mistake because the golems will never rest until they're avenged for that."

A tall man stepped out from behind a dark tapestry and

demanded, "Twenty nine people dead?! What do you mean?!"

"It's all lies!" Marla screamed. "I didn't cause anybody to be killed!"

"She personally stabbed Captain Gyr to death," Z said. "I was there and saw that. She personally poisoned Nake and Judge Mako and she ordered the death of a man called Zho de Dinkard and she caused another to die while trying to himself kill the same Zho de Dinkard half a year earlier. She had twenty four guardsmen trained to kill. They were all killed as they tried to kill other guardsmen to protect her plots and schemes.

"These are only the ones I know about and the golems know about."

"So. Her plans to use the city guard to, as she claimed, `consolidate the city's governing structures,' has resulted in a lot of death," the sorcerer said sadly. "I was afraid something like that would happen. She's always had such plots and plans on her mind."

"You've known her a long time?" Z asked.

"Yes. She's my wife's sister. We were raised together," he answered. "Karla, my wife, warned me she was destined to cause trouble and grief, but I hoped her marriage to Lest would straighten her out. I should have known when their son and daughter came to the islands that it had gone wrong again."

"You have a son and daughter?" Z asked Marla.

"They're staying in another safe place," the sorcerer answered. "I'm glad I didn't reveal where to her. She would have used them.

"I withdraw any and all protection. Do as you must. I sense great power from that shield, that medallion and in those golems she told me about – though she claimed they were from another sorcerer who was jealous of her husband

and was trying to destroy her.

"You see, Marla, I never trusted you. I never believed you. You were never a stable person and such people are dangerous."

He turned and walked stiffly from the room. The golems immediately used a sedative on her and Z used the probe built into his shield. The crystal would be taken to Maita for analysis as the facilities on the shield couldn't do more than record the crystal.

The golems then sprayed her with an instant antidote to the sedative and they started back toward the little town along the coast road. The wind was higher and the rain was driving. They hadn't seen the sorcerer again as they left.

When they reached a fork in the road that led up into the mountains Marla bolted and tried to run up the road, but the golems were floating immediately ahead of her. She doubled back to the coast road where Z waited. She stared him in the eyes a moment, then turned to move on toward the town. It was a few steps later when she again bolted to the cliff edge to jump to her death on the rocks more than a hundred meters below.

"Marla was always rather distant with everyone, including me," Lest said. "We raised our family and they escaped when they were past adolescence to get away from her. She wasn't cruel and she didn't mistreat them when they were small, but they always felt she didn't really care about them. Perhaps she didn't.

"They left because she began to want to control their every move and thought. It got so bad I agreed and sent them to live with Pash, who you met on the island. He didn't tell her they were there, but she learned of it from a person who came through Castiel on his travels.

"Pash sent them away when she again began to try to influence them and him. I would get some messages back and forth, but he wouldn't let me know where they were because she could always find a way to get information from me. I was always easy for her to manipulate, I suppose. It often seemed so much easier if I let her do things her way. The only times we ever had any serious disagreements were concerning the children. I very consciously avoided learning about what she was doing. I quite honestly never considered she would go to Pash. I believed she would avoid him strictly because he had hidden the children from her and because she couldn't control him. That would be the very last place I would think to look for her – which, incidentally, was probably why she went there. She knew I was aware of how very much Pash disliked her.

"It's a sad thing. The saddest part of it is that now I can't really bring myself to grieve for her passing. We were as much as strangers the past fifteen or so years. She went her own route and I went mine. We were cordial to one another, but that was all. She had her part of the house and I had mine. We were more like two people staying in the same inn who would meet by coincidence at meals or at a play.

"I feel nothing. Perhaps I feel some slight relief.

"I prefer to never think of it, but that avails no one. It must be done or there is no lesson learned. Those lessons *must* be learned and they must be remembered. It must never again happen. If there is a strange drift by any person or group away from the normal tenets of a society or a relationship we must be prepared to find and under-stand an explanation."

They were in Gild's Inn sharing cav and sweetcakes. Z had returned to Castiel late in the afternoon for a last visit to the people there to see if things were working as they hoped. Fonz was expected soon. Z was explaining what happened at the island.

"She was an expert at appearing to be other than what she was," Z agreed. "I never thought she'd jump off that cliff. I thought she was the type personality who felt she could bluff her way out of anything and that she would try some clever trick when we were in a place where she could escape. It's really better for all that she's dead. I wouldn't know what to do about her other than to confine her in a criminal's cell."

–Well, I'm glad she jumped! I'd have had to shove her over myself if she hadn't! There ain't no way we could have brought her back here in that stupid boat! It wasn't big enough for us, much less for some woman who was trying to cause trouble!–

+Now, No! Be reasonable. We weren't ever even *in* the boat! We flew above it. The Islands really were beautiful green jewels shown against a background of the clearest blue skies and the rippling dark green waters that stimulate the fine poets to rhapsodic....+

–AHHHHHH, SHUT UP, BLORK BRAIN! I'll rhapsodic you! Why the hells can't you just say they were sort of pretty and let it go at that? Sheesh!–

"Actually they're somewhere between rhapsodic jewels and sort of pretty," Z said, grinning at Lest. "I've found the truth to always be somewhere between what Yes and No say."

"Ah, yes. I see you've learned what Kant was doing when he made them," Lest replied. "As irritating as they can be they present two sides of a problem in such a way one can discern the truth, knowing always that it lies somewhere between the extremes presented."

–Discern the truth?!– No demanded. –How would *you* know the truth if it didn't smack you in the puss, Hose Nose? You don't know what irritating *is* if you haven't shared a few years with Copper Brain here! Talk about a lesson to learn! Try *that* one!–

+Maybe I know a *lit*tle bit about irritation myself, Rattle Mouth!+ Yes snapped, then said, +I'm so sorry! I shouldn't allow him to bother me so. It's because of his deprived childhood. I know he can't help it. It was instilled when we....+

–GEEEYAH! We didn't *have* a childhood, Zilch Brain! In case it escaped your puny excuse for a mind we were *manufactured* in a damned foundry! Cripes!–

"I see the situation, as the famous line goes in the play, is back to normal!" King Fonz said, coming in to take a seat. Viz and Kad were with him.

–How the nine hells would *you* know normal, Turtle Toes?–

"It's whatever you're not, Kirt Plop!" Fonz shot back. "Did you enjoy your little sojourn to the islands?"

+We were just telling our dear friend, Lest, how beautiful those divine islands are, sitting in a sea of tranquil dignity with the cool breezes teasing playfully at....+

–JUST, FOR THIS ONCE, SAY THE HELLS 'YES!' SHEEEEEE!–

"I always liked the islands," Viz said. "The life's easy, but you get lazy."

"I've never been off the land, even in the river," Kad replied. "I'm nervous around water. I've never understood why, but there it is! Some things just are. That's why I always drink beer!

"Gild! A beer, if you will!"

+Wonderful! I see you've both come to understand what happened. That's good. It isn't healthy to brood because of those unhappy things best forgotten. One must not allow depressing....+

–Spirits help me! *Please*! If they're best forgotten why do you continually bring them back to face all of us, Worm Brain? They did what they had to do. Now *let* them forget it!–

"We don't hold on to guilt that's undeserved," Kad answered, grinning at Z. "The great evil would have been to *not* act, which would let that bunch go on killing innocent people. No's right about it. It was something we had to do. It was our duty and responsibility. We didn't have any choice in any of it, but he's wrong about for-getting it. It's very important to remember because we'll never let anything like that get started again so we won't have to stop it when it's already done the damage."

"We had two unpleasant paths we could follow and no other real choices. We took the shortest one, that's all," Viz said. "Neither was a path any rational person would ever choose to be on and that's one fact we will never forget."

"We can hope such a thing is never again necessary," King Fonz agreed. "We'll keep the games and festivals. The training is good for developing skills, but the fact we know those things will hopefully deter others from such sordid schemes.

"Lest has started to write a book. It's a thing you spoke of your first stay here in Castiel. I find it fascinating!"

"About the movement of the stars?" Z asked.

"Yes," Lest replied. "The stars are one part of it. I've discovered that Gaerkt moves around the sun as do at least two other stars, but the most of the stars move in paths that will take a lot of study. I can't find what they're moving around, but very subtle changes in their positions shows they *are* moving."

"Really?" Z asked. "I mean ... that's logical. I suppose if Gaerkt's moving and Selipe's moving and the sun's moving then everything's moving, but the stars always appear to be in the same places at the same time of night to me. They certainly haven't moved *much* in ten years because I watched them for that long."

"I use a long tube with a thin wire across it and a shiny piece of metal," Lest said. "I fixed the tube very firmly after your first trip and found the shadow of the wire was changed very subtly over the year."

"But the shadow would move because everything moves from east to west all the time!" Viz cried.

"I have a theory that Gaerkt itself is turning – much like a ball rolling along – and that the other stars only *seem* to turn, as a result," Lest explained. "It turns toward the east so everything appears to be moving to the west. Don't ask me how such a thing is possible. I have much to study about that!

"I position the wire east to west so the shadow only shows if it moves north or south. I had to take stars such as Yellowblue and The Eye of the Glort, which are very close to overhead, to study. It is very difficult to study those that are not on that line."

"It's all beyond my comprehension," Fonz protested. "I get a bit dizzy merely thinking that Gaerkt itself may be rolling. I like the proof Gaerkt is round. That is something I can be led to understand. Lest proved the shadow of Gaerkt is what causes the phases of the moon."

"Mikill showed me how to understand that," Lest replied. "His old sorcerer friend showed him about shadows. It was only to me to make a position chart that will predict where the phase will be in relation to the sun and to the other stars that move around the sun. My proof those stars and Gaerkt move around the sun and that Selipe moves around Gaerkt proves the fact Gaerkt is a sphere. By logical extension all stars are spheres because the sphere is the perfect natural shape."

"It's all between the top of my head and the ceiling!" Viz complained. "It sounds good, but it also sounds impossible at the same time. I think if Gaerkt's rolling we'd all be thrown off of it. All you have to do is spin your plate and you'll see that everything ends up on the table."

"Ah! You can also attach a rope to a bucket and spin around with the bucket full of water until the bucket is straight out to the side and not one drop of water spills out!" Lest argued triumphantly. "If I can discover *why* I've solved it!"

"But that seems simple! Even I could figure that out if I worked at it," Kad declared.

"That's the tricky part," Z replied. "It sounds so simple and easy, but every time you ask one question you get six more *questions* instead of one answer!

"There is the thing Kant said about the motion of the stars that I find to be too far beyond comprehension because of the numbers involved. For the stars to move so little in our perception over so many years they must be at distances that ... I can't conceive of such distances. There is where a thousand questions come to mind!"

+Kant always taught that. Kant always said answers aren't important. Only questions have meaning.+

"That doesn't make any sense," Fonz said.

"Ah! But it *does*!" Lest cried. "I think Kant was very wise as well as very powerful."

–He was, Boat Butt! He made Yes and me because he said we imply thousands of questions and don't have *any* answers!–

"You got that one right!" Fonz cried. "For once I agree! *You* don't have *any* answers!"

+Heeee! He really got you that time, Negative Noggin!+

"Yugh! Aren't you supposed to be the nice one, Positive Puss?" Z asked.

+I forgot.

+Isn't it wonderful how we can get together and enjoy each others' company without worrying about those problems people cause when they let their own greeds rule their actions?

+I was telling No how good I feel that these horrible things are finally resolved now!

+So! Now, King Fonz, we have promised to bring something to your attention some time ago, but have been distracted by events over which we had no control, so it has had to wait.

+It is also true that Mako and Marla were to bring it to your attention, but I have no reason to believe they ever did. It is, in true point of fact, my personal impression that they were lately intentionally attempting to stop your learning of several small distresses among the people to thus lessen your approval among them. Hopefully that is a thing of the past. We can now mention those things that....+

–What the hells are you talking about, Blither Puss?! By the time you get around to stating your point King Fonz will die of old age!–

+Why, the wash pond. We told them right here that it....+

"Hey! That's right!" Gild exclaimed. She was pouring more hot cav for most of them and had poured another beer for Kad. "We worked out a way to stop all that soap and scum from running by the city."

They spent the rest of the evening discussing various little projects to help make Castiel more modern. It was thoroughly pleasant for all of them.

In the morning Mikill the Traveler and the golems who had attached themselves to him announced they were going to move on, seeking new adventure and knowledge. It was entirely possible they would someday return to Castiel.

The golems were stored in the cargo hold and their computer was turned off. Z was in the pilot's dome in his favorite seat and Heleemius was beside the holovid communications console in the comfortable seat there.

"You were able to do precisely what we all felt was best," Heleemius agreed. "They have a strong cultural and psychological imperative to avoid violence while also having a strong sense of defense against that violence. It's a position we very often have to spend centuries instilling in these kinds of races."

They're naturally a nonviolent people. The basic imperative was there, we only had to stop someone else from changing them away from it.

"I still think the golems' drive computer is intelligent," Z argued stubbornly, taking one of those odd tangents he sometimes did in their conversations. "Their replies are simply too fitting to a situation and too quick for anything else."

"Okay. Change the subject. That's stuff we all agree with anyhow," Heleemius replied, smiling broadly. "The golem driver is definitely intelligent, but in the same way all those ships out there are intelligent. It's not like yours or mine or Maita's."

They're very intelligent, but not cognizant. There isn't any meaningful `I' or `we' with them. They aren't aware.

"Are you sure?" Z asked. "There are times I'm positive they really do despise each other and I know damned well they have emotions about some of the people we meet."

They're programmed to despise each other, or to appear to. Any other emotions they show are expressions of my own about people. I didn't like Nake from the first and I was in control of them at the time, so they were input to react the way I felt. They don't actually feel anything. They have billions of random responses programmed and the drive computers can select any one of them in a few milliseconds. The computers are self-programming. No seldom repeats the same insult in a period of a year and can match the names to the world and language. It's a curiosity I included in the programming of its computer to see if I could. It calculates and remembers the terms and can translate them back and forth among some thousands of languages. It experiments. Some of the things fail, but most are pretty good. I enjoy them.

"No came up with some good ones for Nake," Z said. "Bulge Butt was good, but Adipose Nose was 'way over most people's heads on Gaerkt."

"Yes. I was watching the `Raft Aft' thing," Heleemius agreed. "I liked it, but it was a bit out of context there."

"What I'll never really understand is how those golems always come into a situation or place being so damned visible, then become part of the natural background to the point no one notices them anymore," Z pointed out. "You *do* start liking them."

"It's a fine psychological point and one their computer has

figured to an amazingly close degree," Heleemius replied. "They make themselves extremely visible, vulgar, loud, irritating – everything that draws the attention of any observer, then they seem to disappear when they act more quietly. It's the subtle difference that quickly draws your attention to someone who's consciously trying to be unnoticed while you don't know that person's in the same room with you when they don't seem to be part of whatever's happening at a given time."

Yes. It's an art I'm proud I was able to put into the main computers. They're artificial. They're the same as a lamp or a picture on the wall. You notice the lamp when it's on or you notice the picture when someone says something about it, but at other times, those objects are simply ... there. When they don't do anything deliberately to call attention to themselves, they're another part of the blur of background details. They're the holovid when it's turned off.

"The stark contrast of their normal abrasiveness to those times they're merely there tends to add to it," Z said. "I think the Yes character needs a bit of toning down though. No used to irritate me the most, but lately I'd like to strangle Yes at times!"

That's the point. If Yes is being nicey-nice, as No calls it, it's in the center of your attention and can change the mood of the audience. It can then become the focus of contempt. No's point is then accepted in a sort of psycho-logical revenge. It works the other way when No's being an ass and Yes is being the more practical one.

"They work very well," Heleemius agreed. "I think it would probably be a serious mistake to actually give them intelligence. They'd begin to develop in ways that would surely detract."

Exactly. I can control them precisely when I have to with no resistance. If I need intelligent reactions to the same kinds of situations I can use Tab or Kit or one of the ships.

"Speaking of them, what's happening at home?" Z asked.

We'll be there in a couple of hours. I'll want to stop at Hospital to be sure I calibrated some of my new crap right, then I'll want to stop at University to input a few things I learned into the master teacher there.

"I have to get back to my projects," Heleemius said. "I was interested in what you did here and how you did it. The training of those troops in the particular way you did it was interesting. I didn't think you really understood that much about what was needed there until time for the confrontation at the barracks."

"To be honest about it I didn't," Z admitted. "I tried for a general purpose sort of thing with emphasis on playing games. It was purely good luck they could actually kill anyone. I'd hoped to train them in a way that they'd be incapable of it. You can't begin to know how relieved I was when they did what they did!"

"They're a moral people who were outraged to learn those men actually killed their trainer in cold calculated style simply because someone ordered them to do it," Heleemius replied. "They actually did find themselves in a position of having two great evils to choose between. They saw it as obvious that to *not* act as they did was the greater evil. It was the combination of your teaching and their natural instincts. Later the golems were able to suggest Zho had very deliberately trained them at his great personal disgust to be able to act as they did because Zho was a truly compassionate and moral person. It was accidental good luck *plus* interpretation after the fact. You're known for your phenomenal luck all over the galaxy. Here's another case."

That was true. They chatted for a few minutes, then Heleemius went back to his projects and Maita headed for Hospital.

I input the whole sordid mess into Library and read about what Kurk and Thing did on Hades. I have a crystal of that and one of the exploits of our intrepid detectives for your perusal. TAR One's glad I'm back in charge, but it did a very good job. Things are really running smoothly except for the odd incidents the rest of the crew are keeping tabs on. Theron and Searcher send their regards. Theron's bringing a couple of Zulians and some Parfs to EC to paint. Theron's even talked several of the Woost into coming to collaborate in that. Your very own grandson and great-granddaughter are making quite a name for themselves at University through their research into the nature of universal genetic constants. That's about all.

"With the hints I've received about Thing in Kurk's plane I'm anxious to see what ... my *what*?!" Z said.

Oops! I wasn't supposed to let you know about that part. I'm getting too much like you organics. I think about one thing and talk on about something else and don't even listen to what I'm saying.

"My *what*!?!" Z demanded.

Remember about seventy years ago when Manehel Mothrensthahl Beedeq Verrinaudenen Deegarsenfrag Frashklindrecht Kelthenheimstradtforscht stayed with you in that Maitan marriage thing for four years?

"Of course I remember Bee!" Z said. "She was my *wife*, for Christ's sake!"

Well, it seems she was pregnant when she left EC. She didn't want to continue in the marriage because your interests were so widely divergent and she didn't want to stay on EC. She wanted to go back to Plamaita so she didn't renew the marriage.

"But she was *pregnant*?!" Z cried.

*Yes. Hameshan Frashklindrecht, who stayed with you so much since he was growing into puberty until he died of old age was actually your son. You never called him anything but Ham and never asked his full name, which was Hameshan *Zutec* Nadeschdent Frashklindrecht – Great exploding galaxies! I can never quite understand these interminable Maitan names! Well, I do, but they're downright ridiculous if you ask me! Why should your name have to relate your entire family history?*

"Get to the point!" Z demanded.

Ham was your son, but Bee thought it better you not know because she thought you never made any sense with your stupid ideas about such things. Maitans enter into those four year marriage contracts and can renew them or not according to the situation at the end of the four years. She knew you'd get crazy knowing he was your son because he'd grow old and die while you just went on. He agreed with her so no one ever informed you that you had descendants.

"So! If Ham was my son, then Yolga was my granddaughter and Bar and Hel were my grandsons and Hel is at University along with his daughter Tag!" Z said. "I'll be damned!"

Are you okay?

"Surprisingly, yes," Z replied. "I think I'm past my crazier stages. I think I could have handled it if I'd known. I don't think I could have handled it if my first Maitan wife, Looki, had a kid when *she* left."

Well....

"You're kidding! Say you're kidding!" Z cried.

No. She had a daughter called Teeleshauwn Yuna Kappanateht Nikitrah Zutec Plishterforten who had a son, Kappanateht Zutec Vurnesh Jonvshak Klesterhavenfrendt, who had two kids who each had two kids, one of which had one kid, one didn't ever breed and the others each had two. You can trace all of that with the comps at EC through Plamaita's statistics department.

"Good lord! I thought I was the last of the Zutec line! Now they're all over the whole damned galaxy!" Z said. "I'm surprisingly calm about all that. Maybe I'm even a little proud!"

Well, your luck didn't come through and you don't have too much intelligence, but the mothers' sides had enough that none of them are big disappointments. That's something I guess.

"Hah! Stick it in your focus coils! You just *said* my grandson and great-granddaughter were making a name for themselves!" Z said.

I also said their mothers contributed the intelligent part. We're home!

"It's good to have you back home, Z," Kurk said. "I suppose Maita gave you the crystal about what happened on Hades. I should know by now that anyone with any intelligence doesn't take Thing anywhere!"

They were sitting around Z's patio/terrace watching the yellow sun set with the green one just rising over the mountaintop behind them. There were two Parf artists down by the shore painting the scene.

[Hah! You had more fun than you ever had before! Admit it! We were able to start your stagnant world up and get it moving again! Even you had to admit the only alternative was back to barbarism within a couple of centuries!]

Yes. That seems to be true. I'm getting all kinds of questions about how to run an empire from Hades. Tlorg has Plutons going back and forth all the time. It's a good thing that power plant works in your plane, Kurk. The portal can stay open there. The magnetic shield makes it unlikely enough material will ever pass through from either direction to make a difference. They're maintaining a permanent portal with Targ and one with Frome with the extra power.

Thing climbed from Tab's shoulder to Z's to reach a tentacle into the plate of snacks Maita had placed on the little table there.

"Maita gave us crystals of your little exploit," Kit said. "I think we'll be able to use the golems in a number of things in the future. We're learning the best ways to employ them. They're almost like members of the crew sometimes."

"They make really great spies!" TR agreed over the speakers. "They really do just blend into the background. People tend to forget they're there.

"They're also a lot of fun!"

"Yeah. They held me back from making a couple of big mistakes on Gaerkt," Z said. "I tended to blab on while I was Mikill about things only Zho could possibly have known. I was amazed when Lest didn't notice that."

Lest was too emotionally involved because of his wife. He didn't know which way to turn and he felt guilty because he'd let it go too far and because he felt he let her use him. He still feels responsible for Zho's death.

"According to this crystal he can handle that and will file it as a lesson learned," T Six said. "He'll feel guilty, but he'll also convince himself he couldn't have done anything much differently. He's somewhat a fatalist.

"Do you think his children will get in touch with him again now that she's gone?"

"I think so," Z replied. "Lest will contact Pash and Pash will contact them.

"Maita screwed up and let it slip about me having a bunch of kids and grandkids and more running around. I now know about Hel and his daughter at University. You don't have to hide any of that from me anymore. I can handle it. I already have!"

[I see. Maita's sending that you know about the first bunch, too. I'm glad you know. I always hated hiding that sort of thing from you.]

*At least they're not having to hide from him because he's nuts like Marla's kids hid from her. They don't even *know* he's nuts!*

"Oh, I think most people in the Maitan Empire realize he's a few stars short of a galaxy," Kurk said. "So long as he's not violent we're all willing to sorta overlook it. Remember: we call him our crazy Terran!"

Z jumped from his seat to tackle Kurk. Thing sprung back to stay on the chair.

The object was to hit Kurk and knock him into the pond,

but Kurk is too big to be knocked around that easily. Z slid to the patio floor while Kurk stood still.

"Maybe we won't care if he *does* become violent if that's the best he can do!" Tab noted.

[According to the laws of physics you have to gather far more striking force than that if you're going to move an object as large and heavy as the furry horror, Z. After all this time I'd think you'd learn that!]

"If you want to put Kurk into that pool you have to first *lift*, then thrust!" Tab instructed, grabbing Kurk and shoving him into the pool. Kurk grabbed Tab at the same time and drug him into the pool with him. Z was between them and went in, too, so Kit decided he might as well join them.

They wrestled around in the pool a bit, then came back out dripping. Thing was still perched unconcernedly on the chair nibbling on the snacks. A Woost and a Parf had come to stare at them. They looked at each other, giggled and stepped into the transmat portal to be instantly transported to other parts of EC (or perhaps another planet!).

"Are you receiving that?" TR suddenly asked.

I am.

"Me, too," T Six added. "We asked that all those kinds of things be reported. What should we do?"

It's at several places at once so there's some kind of plan behind it. We're all well-rested. Our last efforts were more a vacation than anything else so let's form a plan and see what this is about!

[I suppose we might as well. I don't imagine any of these clowns are ever going to mature! We can hope not! That would really change the way ... heee!]

This time Thing ended up in the pool with them.

C. D. Moulton's works are available on most major outlets as printed or e-books. CD writes the CD Grimes, PI, mysteries, the Det. Lt. Nick Storie mysteries, the Clint Faraday mysteries, the Flight of the Maita science fiction series, books on orchid culture and many others of many types. Mystery, adventure, intrigue, science fiction, humor, fantasy, paranormal, mild erotica, and factual.